Dear Romance Reader,

Welcome to a world of breathtaking passion and never-ending romance.

Welcome to *Precious Gem Romances*.

It is our pleasure to present *Precious Gem Romances*, a wonderful new line of romance books by some of America's best-loved authors. Let these thrilling historical and contemporary romances sweep you away to far-off times and places in stories that will dazzle your senses and melt your heart.

Sparkling with joy, laughter, and love, each *Precious Gem Romance* glows with all the passion and excitement you expect from the very best in romance. Offered at a great affordable price, these books are an irresistible value—and an essential addition to your romance collection. Tender love stories you will want to read again and again, *Precious Gem Romances* are books you will treasure forever.

Look for eight fabulous new *Precious Gem Romances* each month—available only at Wal★Mart.

Lynn Brown, Publisher

LOVE
SONG

Mary McGuinness

Zebra Books
Kensington Publishing Corp.

http://www.zebrabooks.com

ZEBRA BOOKS are published by

Kensington Publishing Corp.
850 Third Avenue
New York, NY 10022

First Printing: November, 1996
10 9 8 7 6 5 4 3 2 1

Printed in the United States of America

For my father, John J. Gillick,
an extraordinary story teller.

For my mother, Regina Gillick,
who chose to sing lullabies rather than arias.

For my father-in-law, William E. McGuinness,
who could turn any event into a party.

For my mother-in-law, Marguerite McGuinness,
who made the parties happen, and especially for being the
unintentional inspiration for this book!

Chapter One

"Dr. Caldwell, I've just run over your grandmother." Tessa Marcovy leaned her head against the wall of the phone booth and groaned. Too blunt. There had to be a better way to say it.

Muffled but chipper music flowed on relentlessly from the receiver. Good. Still on hold. Still time to find the right words. She shivered. Facing fifty thousand screaming rock fans had never given her jitters like these.

"This is Tessa Marcovy," she said under her breath. "I'm a music therapist at City Hospital. In fact, we've met several times." She shook her head. Too wordy. And very likely to make Dr. Caldwell hang up if he remembered that their brief meetings could be described more accurately as confrontations.

"Dr. Caldwell, this is Tessa Marcovy calling from the emergency room at City Hospital. Your grandmother had a little accident after the concert at the Music Institute."

Too evasive. And could a fractured ankle be considered a little accident in an eighty year old woman?

Tessa closed her eyes and shuddered, once again seeing Flossie Caldwell pinned under the rear wheel of the station wagon, hearing the shrieks of Flossie's elderly friends, feeling her mouth grow dry with sudden panic.

And then . . . a blank. No memory of calling the rescue squad, talking to the police or getting to the hospital. Nothing until she sat in the emergency room cubicle with Flossie, agreeing to notify her grandson, Dr. Samuel Adams Caldwell.

A reluctant chuckle escaped in spite of her worry. Flossie should have told her to contact the grandson she lovingly referred to as Buddy instead of his short-tempered brother. At least she could have achieved her goal of getting Tessa and her grandson together, if only in the emergency room.

The automatic doors leading to the main part of the hospital whooshed open. Tessa turned and saw Dr. Caldwell stride into the waiting room, snowy lab coat flapping, stethoscope bouncing against his starched blue shirt.

Tessa gave the phone a sour glance. "Thanks for nothing," she muttered and slammed the receiver into its cradle.

Dr. Caldwell had already disappeared into the treatment area. Tessa ran after him, anxious to get the initial meeting over. She found him at the chart rack behind the nurses' station, flipping through the metal binders.

"Dr. Caldwell," she began.

He whirled around at the sound of her voice. "Where the devil is Florence Caldwell? What . . ." His voice trailed off and his shaggy blond eyebrows snapped together. "I'm sorry, but family members aren't allowed in this area. Go back to the waiting room until you're called."

A wave of annoyance washed away Tessa's anxiety. The man was the biggest jerk this side of the Mississippi. They'd met at least four times and he still couldn't remember her.

She fished in her purse and pulled out her hospital ID badge.

"I'm authorized, and here with your grandmother as well."

He flicked a glance at her badge and gave her a distant smile. "Ah, yes. The music lady." He turned back to the chart rack and pulled out a metal clipboard. "My sparring partner in the staff newsletter's coverage of the proposed budget cuts." Flipping the chart open, he scanned the pages rapidly.

"So you've already heard that some idiot ran over my grandmother. The hospital grapevine must be working overtime." He took her arm and turned her toward the waiting room. "Nice of you to stop by, Miss Marcovy, but right now she needs medical treatment. So why don't you take your jingle bells and cheery tunes and find a patient who needs amusement rather than medical intervention?"

Annoyance escalated to anger. Sam Caldwell's patronizing manner made Tessa yearn for a dark alley and a blunt instrument.

She glared at him. "Because I'm the idiot, that's why!"

Dr. Caldwell was paging through his grandmother's chart again. "No, no," he said absently, "some people actually believe that music therapy may have beneficial effects." He continued reading. "Non-displaced fracture of the malleolus."

Dr. Caldwell's satisfied nod, Tessa knew, had nothing to do with music therapy and everything to do with his grandmother's relatively minor injury.

Tessa snatched the chart from his hands. "Let me be more precise. I'm the idiot who ran over your grandmother."

That statement caught his attention. Sam leveled an icy stare at her, a look that had served him well in his military

career. More than once it had wilted some incompetent
fool into a stammering, self-excusing wreck.

Tessa Marcovy merely stared back at him, her slate gray
gaze never shifting from his.

"You ran over my grandmother?" He clipped each word
off and continued to stare at Tessa, waiting for an explanation.

She didn't offer one, but her creamy skin suddenly
matched the color of her unbusiness-like pink suit. Sam
wondered briefly why on earth she was dressed like a character in a 1940's movie.

The suit's heart-shaped neckline and nipped-in waist
were a startling contrast to the lab coats and scrubs of the
hospital workers. A lace handkerchief peeped from the
breast pocket. Frivolous pink sandals added several much-
needed inches to her height.

The final straw was Tessa's black hair, confined by something that reminded Sam of a miniature fishing net—a
net that was pink, silky, and dotted with little roses. It
was in the same class as her lace handkerchief and shoes.
Perfectly practical items ruined by a lot of fluff. And those
were just the things he could see. Sam had a hunch that
the petal soft material of her suit wasn't hiding sensible
white cotton underwear.

His jaw tightened with disapproval. Ms. Marcovy's
clothes, like her profession, were totally out of place in
the high tech atmosphere of the emergency room.

Tessa raised her chin a notch. "Dr. Caldwell, if you're
trying to intimidate me, you've got a long, tedious evening
ahead of you." She thrust the clipboard back at him and
he grabbed it without thinking. "As for me, I outgrew
playing 'Statues' years ago, so I'm going to check on your
grandmother. Feel free to join us when it's convenient."

Tessa brushed past him, her flared skirt swirling around

an undeniably alluring pair of legs. Her high heels tapped briskly down the hall.

Sam caught up with her just before she entered a curtained cubicle. "Wait a minute. I want some answers."

Tessa turned to face him, neatly netted hair swinging over one shoulder.

"Then ask some questions." Tessa suggested.

Sam took a deep breath. "How did my grandmother . . ." His voice trailed off as a faint scent of roses reached him.

"Go on," she encouraged him.

"What the hell is that?" He reached out and touched one of the little blossoms on the pink silky thing.

"It's a snood." Tessa flipped her hair away from his hand. "And frankly, Dr. Caldwell, as much as I'd like to discuss women's hair accessories with you, I think your grandmother's accident has priority."

"I couldn't agree more. So if you'll stop trying to distract me, maybe we can make some progress." Sam didn't mean to raise his voice, but his patience was running thin.

"I'm trying to distract you?"

An unladylike snort took Sam by surprise.

"At least I'm not doing it on purpose, which is more than I can say about your attempts to intimidate me."

Sam's hand closed over Tessa's wrist before she could pull the white curtain aside.

"The only thing I'm attempting to do is wring some information from you, Ms. Marcovy. Without success, I might add. And if I was trying to intimidate you, trust me, you would be."

"I wouldn't count on it." The silvery voice from behind the curtain was rich with amusement. "There's only one thing she's afraid of, Buddy, and it's not you."

Tessa's hand and jaw dropped simultaneously. "Buddy?" The anger simmering in her smoky eyes vanished and was replaced by amused disbelief. "You're Buddy?"

"It's a nickname," Sam said defensively. "Do you have a problem with that?"

Tessa's innocent smile didn't fool Sam. She was enjoying his discomfort.

"Of course not," she assured him. "It's adorable."

Sam could have sworn Tessa chuckled as she stepped into the examination room.

"Sunshine, you're back!"

". . . been gone a long time . . ."

"So you found Buddy . . ."

"How do you like . . ."

". . . a real hunk, Sunshine!"

The chorus of elderly voices that greeted Tessa made the short hairs on the back of Sam's neck stand at attention. His grandmother wasn't alone in there. He wondered how many of her matchmaking cronies he would have to face.

Knowing that the best defense was a bold attack, he set his jaw and whisked the curtain aside.

"Buddy!"

Four sunny smiles greeted him.

"Thank goodness you're here!"

Four pairs of innocent eyes beamed at him.

"What an evening!"

Four eager tongues started wagging.

". . . first part was lots of . . ."

". . . nobody's fault, though . . ."

". . . lovely people at this hospital . . ."

". . . poor Sunshine . . ."

Over in the corner stood Tessa, apparently unfazed by the overlapping conversations that made Sam feel like a drowning man with no life preserver in sight.

"Ladies! Quiet!" Blessed silence descended on the room. Sam cocked an eyebrow in his grandmother's direction. "Okay, Gran, 'fess up. How'd you sneak your pals in here?"

"Why, Buddy, what a thing to say!" Flossie Caldwell clicked her tongue reprovingly. "When have I ever resorted to trickery?"

"Any time you can't get what you want legitimately."

Flossie gave Sam an audacious grin. "Regular channels worked fine today. I explained the situation." She folded her age-spotted hands on the white blanket covering her lower body. "I told them that I was afraid to be here alone." A pathetic quaver crept into her voice. "And that Ellen and Hannah and Marge would keep me company and be as quiet as mice . . ."

"Did you tell anybody that you were my grandmother?"

"I may have mentioned it." Flossie squinted her blue eyes thoughtfully. "Come to think of it, I guess I might have told them how unhappy you'd be if you knew I was scared and lonely."

Tessa bit back a grin. She could just imagine the reaction to that statement. Nobody wanted to cross Eagle Eye Caldwell—or his grandmother, Tessa was sure.

The Caldwells had helped found St. Swithin's more than a century ago, and had continued to be major benefactors. More than a few had been attending physicians as well. In her less charitable moments, Tessa wondered how much Sam's last name had to do with his election to the St. Swithin's board as an at-large staff representative.

"You're incorrigible, Gran." Sam folded back the blanket and unfastened the immobilizer that covered her right leg from ankle to mid-thigh.

Tessa flinched at the sight of the elderly woman's ankle, red and swollen. She closed her eyes and held her breath as Sam bent over the damaged leg, steeling herself for the cry of pain that was sure to come. All she heard was a soft exhalation. Could it be a sigh of relief?

She opened her eyes. Flossie relaxed against the hospital bed, evidently undisturbed by Sam's hands moving gently over the injury, long blunt fingers probing and testing. Fine golden hairs dusted the back of his large hands and glimmered under the bright overhead lights.

Magic hands, Tessa thought suddenly. Incredible that such practical, hardworking hands could touch so softly, glide so smoothly, soothe so surely. A brief vision of Sam's hands on her flashed into Tessa's mind and was gone, almost before she could register a mental protest against such an inappropriate thought.

"You'll have to be on a walker for a number of weeks, but it could have been much worse." Sam straightened and pulled the blanket up over his grandmother's legs again. "Want to tell me how the hell this happened?"

Bedlam broke out once again as all four ladies spoke up.

"It wasn't anybody's fault . . ."

"Tessa wanted to pick us up at the entrance . . ."

"But we wanted to walk . . ."

"So then, we all got in . . ."

"And Tessa thought Flossie had shut her door . . ."

"But it wasn't, you see, because I . . ."

"Because Hannah's coat got caught in her door, so she . . ."

"So I opened and reclosed my door . . ."

"And then Sunshine started the car and the wheel sort of ran over my foot . . ."

"And Sam, guess what! She lifted the car off Flossie's . . ."

". . . my ankle took a funny twist when I fell out . . ."

". . . just like those Reader's Digest stories. It's adrenaline or something . . ."

". . . police came and they didn't think it was her fault either, Sam . . ."

"... didn't give her a ticket ..."

"Sunshine went in the ambulance with Flossie ..."

"... ambulance folks thought Sunshine might be too upset ..."

"... to drive, so a nice policeman brought us here ..."

"... and don't you be mad or we'll never speak to you again."

Sam clapped his hands over his ears and grinned in spite of himself. "An empty threat if I ever heard one."

Tessa tried to maintain her air of calm self-assurance but failed. Her lips trembled as she attempted to block out the mental pictures conjured up by her elderly defenders. Her head pounded and iron bands seemed to squeeze her chest. Beads of sweat pearled her forehead while a roaring sound filled her ears.

Tessa gulped a deep breath, willing herself to look at Sam, sure that the smile she had seen was directed only at his grandmother, not her. Her heart sank. She was right. Sam was frowning, his blue eyes intent on her.

"Has anybody looked at you yet?" he asked roughly.

Tessa shook her head. "Of course not. Your grandmother was the only one injured."

"Better let me check you over. You look pretty shocky."

The thought of Sam bending over her, listening to her heart, curling those magic fingers around her wrist in search of her pulse, was enough to send a shot of adrenaline surging through Tessa. She straightened and mustered up what she hoped was a confident laugh.

"Don't be silly. I'm fine." She gave him the smile. The one that had captivated audiences all over the United States. "Cross my heart." Tessa turned up the wattage on the smile and traced her forefinger over the lace handkerchief in her breast pocket.

She was gratified when Sam blinked and took a step closer to her. Whatever else she had lost, the smile still

worked. Pressing her advantage, she turned toward Flossie's friends.

"I'll get my car and take you home, ladies. They must
be wondering why you're so late."

Flossie raised her hand, cutting off three simultaneous
replies.

"I had a sweet nurse call Bellefontaine and ask for the
van to come and pick them up." She glanced at the clock
on the wall. "I hope somebody lets us know when it
arrives."

Tessa seized the opening. "I'll walk them to the door
and wait until it does." She took Flossie's hand and smiled.
"You should have some time alone with . . ." she flicked
an innocent smile in Sam's direction. "Buddy."

She was rewarded by a reluctant laugh. So, the rumors
were wrong. Eagle Eye Caldwell did have a sense of humor
after all. Too bad. It made him almost likeable.

Flossie clutched Tessa's hand. "Promise you'll come
back and say good night before you leave, Sunshine."

"Flossie, you need rest." Once she escaped from Sam's
disturbing presence, she was planning on a clean getaway.

"Please, dear." The grip on her hand tightened.

"I'm sure your grandson would rather have you to himself."

"I'd rather have my grandmother happy." Sam was leaning against the wall, arms crossed over his chest, amusement evident in his eyes.

"Then I'll come back." Darned if she'd let Sam Caldwell
think he was getting under her skin. Even if he was. "Come
on, ladies." Tessa pulled the curtain aside. "Let's go before
the van driver gets here and decides you've already left."

With a flurry of kisses, admonitions to get some sleep
and promises of daily visits, the three friends filed out of
the room. Tessa waved and followed them, her pink skirt
once again twirling in a most distracting way.

"Doesn't she have pretty legs, Buddy?"

"I didn't notice," he lied.

Flossie chuckled. "Tell it to the marines, flyboy."

"Gran, you're something else." Sam pulled a stool next to the bed and sat down. "And I'm not a flyboy right now."

"But you're trying to be." She fixed him with the same gimlet gaze that had always pried the truth out of him when he was growing up.

"I'm not trying, Gran. I'm going back to my reserve unit as soon as I can convince the Air Force that my back is completely healed and ready for action." He set his jaw defensively. "And don't tell me I'm crazy."

"Never." Flossie patted his cheek affectionately. "If jumping out of airplanes with sixty-five pounds of medical supplies on your back makes you happy, then I say go for it, no matter how bizarre it seems to the rest of the world."

"Never mind me, Flossie." He gave her a hard stare. "How the hell did this accident really happen? I don't like you driving with someone who's so far into the ozone that she can't keep her mind on what she's doing."

Flossie's thick white eyebrows snapped together in a fair approximation of Sam's own scowl.

"I hope you're not referring to Sunshine in that smart-alec tone, Samuel."

Samuel. Uh-oh. Sam had the uncomfortable sensation that he had just shrunk two feet and regressed twenty-five years.

His grandmother swept on majestically. "Would you be happier if she had fainted and left me lying on the ground? If she was having hysterics in the waiting room would it help? Would you have handled things any better?"

"I'd never have gotten into the situation."

"Of course you wouldn't," his grandmother agreed with cheerful sarcasm. "You'd never volunteer to take the four of us to a concert. And if by some miracle you did, I'd like to see how you'd deal with Ellen, Hannah and Marge chattering non-stop in your ear and giving you hints on driving."

Sam bit back a grin. His grandmother was right. He wouldn't be caught dead at a concert and would rather be shot than drive Hell's Grannies more than a block.

"The policeman said that it's a very common accident in public parking lots. And besides, it's none of your business. If I'm not angry, why should you be?"

"Okay, okay!" Sam held his hands up in a gesture of defeat. "I know when to make a strategic retreat." And he also knew that the featherheaded Ms. Marcovy would never drive his grandmother anyplace again. He'd see to that!

"Good." Flossie relaxed against the pillow, a broad smile on her face. "At least one good thing has come out of this."

Sam raised an eyebrow quizzically. "And that is?"

"You finally met Sunshine." Flossie beamed at him. "Isn't she everything I said?"

Warning alarms sounded in Sam's brain and a premonitory shiver ran down his spine. "I don't know. What did you say?"

"Oh, Buddy!" Flossie clicked her tongue. "I've been talking about her for the past two months. Don't you listen?"

"Not when you're cooking up one of your matchmaking schemes." Sam figured a little brutal honesty wouldn't hurt. "And that's what you've got in mind, right?"

"Well . . ." Flossie lowered her eyes and plucked a loose thread on her hospital gown.

The full realization finally sank in. Sam stared at his grandmother incredulously. "Me and a music therapist?" Sam rested his hand on Flossie's forehead. "Hmm. Not feverish. Maybe I should call the psych department for a consult."

Flossie tapped Sam's knee with her forefinger. "You're afraid to take her out! Oh, I've read the articles you two have written for the staff newsletter. You think music therapy is dumber than dirt, and she thinks you're a gung-ho surgeon who wants to cure everything with a scalpel." Her blue eyes twinkled at him. "You're scared that she'll talk you into a big budget increase for music therapy instead of a major cut."

"Our professional differences have nothing to do with it, Gran. It's my damned crazy schedule." Sam sighed and rubbed the heels of his palms against his eyes. "I don't have time for a serious relationship, no matter how special the woman."

Even one whose captivating smile was more alluring than her curvaceous body. Even one whose enigmatic grey eyes made him want to find out what caused the wariness lurking in their depths. Even one whose mere memory made his body tighten.

"Did I use the word serious?" Flossie's china blue eyes sparked with amusement. "Don't flatter yourself. Sunshine doesn't want anything permanent either, you know."

Perversely, this information annoyed Sam. "Why not? And why the hell do you call her Sunshine instead of Tessa?"

Flossie shrugged. "The same reason I call you Buddy instead of Sam. It just fits better. She really is such a ray of sunshine in so many lives."

Sam shook his head. "You should have been a Russian novelist. Too many names to remember."

"Anyway," Flossie continued, ignoring Sam's comment, "you're not the only one with a full life. Besides her work here, she volunteers with our senior citizen choir and a children's group, and . . . oh, tons of stuff! She'd be a perfect date, Buddy. One who could understand your crazy schedule."

When Sam failed to respond, Flossie poked him. "Go on, loosen up and have a fling. Or did you take a vow of celibacy when you joined that Air Force rescue team?"

"What a thing for an eighty year old grandma to say!" Sam's reluctant laugh weakened his protest.

"Oh, grow up, Buddy. I'm old, not dead." Flossie's expression turned meditative. "In fact, there's this gentleman at Bellefontaine . . ."

"God help the poor man! He doesn't stand a chance."

The curtain swished open and Tessa walked in, smiling. "What a noisy pair! I could hear you way down the hall!"

"Well, laughter is the best medicine, Sunshine."

Tessa perched at the end of the hospital bed and took Flossie's hand in hers. "Then you must be almost healed."

Sam wondered if Tessa had any idea how tempting she looked from his vantage point at the head of Flossie's bed. One of Tessa's long legs was tucked under her, while the other swung gently back and forth, the toe of her pink shoe barely brushing the floor. She was listening intently to his grandmother, concern lighting her eyes.

Tessa leaned closer to Flossie and her suit jacket shifted, giving Sam a tantalizing peek at something pink and lacy. Definitely not white cotton.

Sam told himself that he could look away, now that his intellectual curiosity had been satisfied, but his eyes kept sliding back to the tempting shadow between Tessa's breasts.

Maybe Flossie was right. It might do him good to break out of his rut. Who better to relax with than another health care professional? Even one on the far fringes of medicine.

Sam brightened at a sudden thought. Perhaps he could show Tessa that cutting the music therapy budget was regrettable, but logical, considering the hospital's financial situation.

And maybe if he scaled back on the intensity of his

workouts, his body would recharge itself and be more responsive when he went back to a rigorous training program.

"He'd love to, wouldn't you, Buddy?"

"What would I love to do?"

"Drive Sunshine to her car. We just realized that it's still at the Music Institute."

Sam opened his mouth to say no, but Tessa spoke first.

"Absolutely not." She shook her head decisively. "It's not that far. And," she added, guessing Flossie's next objection, "the shuttle bus is still running, so I won't have to walk."

Sam glanced down at Tessa's impractical pink shoes. His gaze once again drifted up the length of her slender legs, past the waist that made him wonder if his hands could span it, and stopped short at the neckline of her suit. Another quick flash of pink lace as Tessa bent to kiss Flossie good night and Sam's sense of self-preservation vanished.

"Come on," Sam said lazily, unfolding himself from the stool. "Why wait for the shuttle when I'm parked right outside?"

Tessa looked at him dubiously.

"You know what the shuttle schedule is like at this time of night." He watched as that shot hit home.

She hesitated, but shook her head again. "No, thanks."

"Maybe you're right, Sunshine. You and Buddy would probably spend the whole ride trying to change each other's minds about the budget appropriations."

His grandmother, Sam reflected, was amazing. She could teach a graduate course in mind manipulation, thought control and reverse psychology. He watched Tessa's expression waver and change from stubborn refusal to sudden speculation as she absorbed the possibilities raised by Flossie's comment.

"Suit yourself," Sam said indifferently. "I'm leaving anyway and I go right by the Music Institute on my way home."

"If you're sure . . ." Tessa sounded hesitant, but Sam knew she had made up her mind.

"No problem." She'd probably kill him when they got to the parking lot, but what the hell—life without a little danger was pretty dull.

Tessa retrieved a small purse from a hook on the wall and swung the strap over her shoulder. "I'll wait for you outside." She blew Flossie a kiss, waved, and left.

Sam gave his grandmother's shoulder an affectionate squeeze.

"You're sure you don't want me to stay here until they get you settled in a room?"

Flossie's eyes twinkled affectionately. "Come on, Buddy, I'm a doctor's widow. I know they're keeping me here overnight to make sure that little chest pain I had in the ambulance was nothing more than stress. Tomorrow morning they'll decide that I'm fine, put me in a cast, and boot me out. Tessa already said she'll take me home."

"Robert Jones dressing, not a cast," Sam corrected, still eyeing her dubiously. "And no way is anybody taking you home but me."

"Control freak." Flossie patted Sam's cheek. "Now get going and take Tessa home! After all the trouble it took to get you and Sunshine together, I don't want you hanging around me instead of her."

Sam shook his finger at her. "Don't start naming your great grandchildren. I'm just giving her a lift to the parking lot."

Flossie flipped her hands at him. "Shoo! Before Sunshine changes her mind and walks. And it wouldn't kill you to get her a bite to eat."

"Uh-uh." Sam shook his head. "I'd get indigestion listening to why her department's budget shouldn't be cut and it would be your fault for planting the idea in her head."

"Don't be a chump, Buddy. You better hope you can make her understand your point of view, or this is one fight you're going to lose. Sunshine knows most of the budget committee members and she's a very persuasive woman."

"I'll take my chances." Sam bent and dropped a kiss on his grandmother's forehead. "Good night, Gran. I'll see you before rounds tomorrow."

"Buddy?" Flossie's questioning voice stopped Sam at the doorway. "You *do* have your car, don't you?"

Sam shook his head, raised a finger to his lips, and winked.

"You rascal." A wicked grin lit Flossie's face. "See you tomorrow."

Sam ducked through the curtain and scanned the corridor for Tessa. She wasn't there. He frowned, surprised by the sudden disappointment that flashed through him.

He strode down the hall toward the waiting room. Through the glass doors leading to the parking lot, he saw a glimpse of pink. Sam nodded with satisfaction. This was going to be fun.

Chapter Two

"That's my ride to the parking lot?'' Tessa looked at the obscenely large motorcycle, its black paint and chrome trim glittering under the parking lot lights.

"Yeah, this is it,'' Sam replied. Opening a saddlebag mounted on the back of the motorcycle, he pulled out a leather jacket and tossed it over the handlebars. He took off his white lab coat, folded it meticulously and stowed it away. Loosening his striped silk tie, Sam unfastened the top button of his oxford cloth shirt and rolled up his sleeves.

"Oh, boy,'' he groaned, stretching his arms over his head and arching his back. "It's been one hell of a day.'' Sam shrugged into the leather jacket, zipped it, and slung one leg over the saddle of the motorcycle. "Come on,'' he said, patting the space behind him. "Let's get going.''

Tessa tried to memorize every detail of this amazing transformation: frosty, buttoned-down Samuel Adams Caldwell had changed before her eyes into this devil may care, leather clad . . .

She searched for the right word.

Hunk.

That was it—a biker hunk.

Sam pulled a black and silver helmet from its rack and tucked it under his arm.

Tessa sucked in a breath as black leather shifted and strained to accommodate the movements of his broad shoulders. She mentally amended her previous assessment.

Not just a hunk.

An ultra hunk.

A world class hunk.

A hunk-o-rama.

Tessa couldn't wait to see her female co-workers. The ones who joked that Dr. Caldwell probably went mountain climbing in a blue oxford cloth parka with a navy and red striped tie and wing-tip hiking boots. They'd either die of envy or think she was hallucinating.

"Come on, climb aboard."

Sam's voice snapped her back to reality. "Thanks," she said, gesturing to her skirt, "but I'll take the shuttle."

"What's the problem? The bike rides two and I've got an extra helmet." He grinned suddenly. "And my grandmother would assure you I'm harmless."

Then why was her heart beating a calypso rhythm? She looked from Sam to the motorcycle. Man and machine looked disturbingly similar—big, powerful, and risky.

Tessa shoved the thought back into her subconscious. "I'll take the shuttle," she repeated.

Sam peered over Tessa's shoulder and shook his head. "Not unless you're willing to wait another hour."

Tessa looked just in time to see the bus pull away from the emergency room entrance. "Oh, no!" She muttered a fine, stress-relieving Hungarian phrase and cast a withering glance over her shoulder at Sam.

"Good night, Dr. Caldwell." She hitched her purse strap over her shoulder and headed toward the street.

"Hey!" Sam protested. "You can't walk to your car alone."

"Watch me." She marched toward the street, waving to the guard in the gate house as she left the parking lot. Behind her, an engine roared into life. Tessa lengthened her stride and wished fervently for track shoes instead of pink high heels.

The motorcycle's full-throated roar sank to a muted growl just behind her, but Sam didn't speak.

He was waiting, Tessa thought, for her to look around. Well, let him wait. She wouldn't give Flossie's exasperating grandson the satisfaction of noticing him. Not a glance, she told herself. Not even the tiniest peek.

She turned around. The man's head was completely covered by a helmet with a mirrored visor. For one panicky moment, Tessa wasn't sure it was Sam. A second glance reassured her. She might not be able to see his face, but those incredible shoulders were a dead give-away.

"Okay, why are you following me?"

Sam raised the helmet's face visor. "I was hoping you'd come to your senses." His blond hair was still hidden, giving his craggy features a harsh look. "This isn't the safest time or place to be walking alone."

Tessa snorted. "Safer than a motorcycle with you."

Sam pulled up next to her. "What did you say?"

"Nothing." She turned and walked away. Once again Sam kept pace with her.

"Come on," Sam said. "Satisfy my curiosity. How come a ride to the Institute is okay in a car but not on a motorcycle?"

Tessa kept on walking.

"It doesn't make sense," he said, "unless you're afraid."

Tessa was sure that Sam's proverbial eagle eyes could

see the flood of color rushing into her cheeks. She was right.

"That's it, isn't it? You're scared!"

Yes, Tessa thought, she *was* scared. Scared of reopening wounds that had finally started to heal. Scared of Sam's reaction if she told him the truth.

She tried to picture the scene. *No, Sam, I'm not afraid of motorcycles. In fact, I owned one back when I was singing with* Uprising. *That's right, the rock group.*

Tessa suppressed a shudder at the thought. She was well aware of Sam's views about her profession. Flossie's accident couldn't have improved his overall impression of music therapists, she was sure. And finding out that she had been a rock singer would only serve to confirm that opinion.

No, for now she was better off letting Sam assume she was afraid of motorcycles. It was much easier than the alternative.

She glanced over her shoulder at Sam. "Of course I'm afraid. Motorcycles are dangerous."

"Oh, lord, not that old line." Sam groaned and shook his head. "Motorcycles are inanimate, incapable of being safe or unsafe. It's the driver that makes a motorcycle dangerous."

"Exactly."

"What does 'exactly' mean?"

Tessa gave an exasperated sigh and stopped walking. "Just look at you! You could be the poster boy for "Daredevils Anonymous," which is what half the hospital staff thinks you are since you broke your back in that rescue mission last year."

"And the other half?" Sam was laughing, clearly not displeased by the notion.

"Thinks you're crazy if you go back to your reserve unit

when you could be on the fast track to Chief of Orthopedics.''

Sam's eyebrows snapped together. "What's your opinion?''

Tessa grinned. "That you're a crazy daredevil.''

"Am I?'' One eyebrow slid up. "First, most people don't understand that I joined the pararescue unit because it was a great place to use my medical and physical skills to help people in crisis situations. Second, the term 'broken back' is vague and inaccurate. I fractured several vertebrae and they are now healed. Third, I want to get back to my unit and I can't do that until I'm able to pass their physical. Therefore, I get physical therapy on a regular basis and I do things on my own time that challenge my skills. And fourth, if you really think I'm crazy, then I'll stop offering you a ride home.''

Sam pushed up his jacket cuff and peered at his watch. "In about forty-five minutes a nice, safe, four-wheeled shuttle will be here, with a nice, sane driver, so go back to the hospital and wait.''

Sam flipped the visor over his face and twisted something on the handlebar. The engine's growl escalated to a full-throated roar as the motorcycle leaped forward. Tessa's breath caught in her throat when Sam leaned at a precarious angle and dragged one foot along the pavement while turning the front wheel. He waved a black gloved hand and took off at a speed that left skid marks on the pavement.

"What an idiot!'' Tessa muttered. "'Go back to the emergency room and wait.' Ha!'' She watched Sam until he was out of sight and then started off towards the Music Institute. She could walk there in ten minutes, she told herself, on streets that were regularly patrolled by the police.

A cloud blotted out the moon and the cool breeze made

her think longingly of a hot bath and an even hotter cup of tea.

"Head up, shoulders back, brisk stride, confident look." Tessa wondered why something that sounded so convincing in her self defense class seemed less plausible when walking alone on an urban street at midnight.

She breathed a sigh of relief when she caught sight of the traffic signal at Euclid Avenue. Once across the busy street, she wouldn't have far to go.

Relief changed to dismay as she got closer to the intersection. It was flooded. Water gushed from a gaping hole in the middle of the street, a swift brown river threatening to escape the confines of the gutters despite the best efforts of the water department workers.

Tessa didn't hesitate. The lure of home, a bath, a cup of tea, and bed was simply too strong. She bent down, slipped off her shoes and headed for the street.

"Hold it, young lady." The voice was kind, but the grip on her arm was uncompromising. "You can't cross here."

"You know," Tessa said, "I'm getting pretty tired of people telling me what I can't do." Turning around, she saw blue serge, brass buttons, and a gold shield. A cop. She tilted her head back and looked into a lined face whose expression told her that this was one man who couldn't be reasoned with, cajoled, or wheedled. Still, no harm in trying.

Tessa gave him a winning smile. "My car is at the Music Institute, officer, so I have to cross at this intersection. It'll ruin my pantyhose, but I don't mind."

The cop folded his arms across his sizeable stomach and stared down at her. "Yeah, well, I mind. You can't go waltzing through that mess in your bare feet."

Her first impression had been right. The officer wasn't dazzled by the clarity of her logic or the warmth of her smile.

"So," he continued, "as I see it, you've got two choices. You can cross Euclid at another intersection if you don't mind walking a few more blocks all by yourself late at night. Or you can make the sensible choice." He turned her around and patted her shoulder. "Head back to St. Swithin's and wait for the shuttle bus. It'll be along in about forty minutes or so."

Tessa opened her mouth, looked up at him, and shut it again.

He nodded. "Good decision," he told her. "I just hate arguments. They make me real cranky."

Tessa smiled ruefully and steadied herself with one hand on his arm while she slipped her shoes on. "I can't believe I'm giving up without a fight. I must be getting old."

"Or sensible," Officer Black suggested.

"Oh, no!" Tessa made a face. "That's even worse."

Suddenly she heard a familiar sound. Tessa turned. Sam was speeding down the street like a knight in leather armor on a black and chrome charger. He stopped well away from the rising water, vaulted off the motorcycle and strode over to Tessa.

"Another offer of a ride?" Tessa asked wearily.

"No." Sam raised his visor and glared at her. "It's not."

"You know this guy?" The policeman jerked a thumb at Sam.

"Yes, and if his offer was still open, I'd accept." Tessa's shoulders sagged. "I'm too tired to refuse."

"This isn't an offer," Sam repeated. "It's an order. Get on the damned bike. I'm taking you to your car."

"Be sure she puts on a helmet," the officer advised Sam.

"Oh, come on," Tessa protested. "I don't need one for such a short trip."

Sam shook his head. "Wrong. I'm sure the officer will agree that only a crazy person would ride without one." He gave Tessa an *I gotcha* smirk.

"Right you are!" The cop clapped Sam on the shoulder. "Keep an eye on this girl, son. You know what she tried to do? Wade across that flooded street in her stocking feet! She could have cut herself or stepped in a hole or done God knows what."

"Doesn't surprise me," Sam said. "She's a real dare-devil."

If looks could kill, Tessa reflected, she'd be under arrest for homicide.

"Well, try to keep her under control for the rest of the night." The cop waved good-bye and strolled back, chuckling, toward the intersection.

Tessa looked at Sam. "You really enjoyed that, didn't you?"

"Yeah," Sam admitted, "I sure did."

She tried to be indignant, but fatigue and the twinkle in Sam's eyes broke down her defenses and she laughed instead. "If that poor cop only knew what you're really like!"

"Let's not start that again." He pulled the extra helmet from the back of the bike and handed it to her.

Tessa took it and replaced it on the rack. "Ohio law doesn't require helmets."

"Caldwell's law does, though. You haven't seen what concrete can do to the cranium. I have." Sam retrieved the helmet and tried to put it on Tessa. She shrieked and ducked.

"Wait a minute," she said, and slid the pink silky thing from her hair. "It took me so long to crochet this snood—I don't want it ruined."

Sam barely heard her. He was concentrating on the drift of black waves that cascaded over Tessa's shoulders and down her back. She looked different with her hair loose—wilder and more exotic. Sam had the distinct impression that he had seen her somewhere before.

He searched his brain for the connection, but was distracted by the blue-black shimmer of Tessa's hair blowing in the breeze, tempting him to tangle his fingers in it.

Sam lifted one hand without thinking, and as quickly dropped it to his side, reminding himself that like everything else about Tessa, her hair was completely impractical. Too long, too thick, too . . . fluffy!

It must be a terrible nuisance to care for, taking hours of time that could be spent in more productive ways. She'd be better off with short hair, he reflected, a feminine version of his own wash and wear cut.

Like hell she would. Sam pushed the thought out of his mind and focused his attention on getting Tessa back to her car as quickly as possible.

Tessa folded the snood, taking care not to crush the silk rosebuds, and slipped it in her purse.

"Okay," she said. "I'm as ready as I'll ever be." She reached for the helmet, but Sam settled it on her head himself. He pulled it down and brushed her hair back so he could fasten the chin strap securely. The scent of roses wafted toward him and he had to restrain himself from leaning over and inhaling the fragrance, a scent that reminded him of a moonlit garden.

Not that he had ever walked through a moonlit garden, but somehow he knew it would smell just like Tessa, warm, fragrant, and intoxicating.

Tessa shook her head tentatively, as if testing the weight of the unfamiliar headgear. "I don't think this is going to be a hot fashion accessory this year. Do I look as weird as I feel?"

She looked, Sam thought, anything but weird. Cute was the first word that sprang to mind. *And sexy as hell.* There it was again, that damned internal commentator, coming up with a completely irrelevant thought.

"You look fine." Sam quickly pulled down his visor and mounted the motorcycle. "Let's go."

The motorcycle shifted, then settled and Sam felt the warmth of Tessa's body pressed against his back. He made the mistake of looking down.

Tessa's nylon clad legs cradled his thighs. Long legs. Sleek legs. Legs that could launch a thousand fantasies. Like the one he was having right now, a fantasy of lace garters. Produced, no doubt, by his overwrought imagination in response to those sensational legs. Closing his eyes, Sam shook his head to clear his mind. He opened his eyes. It wasn't a fantasy. Incomprehensibly, the garters were still there.

Sam was baffled. Surely no modern woman wore stockings, let alone white lace garters to hold them up. Garters that practically dared a man to slip his fingers under those scraps of satin and lace and slide them off Tessa's perfect legs.

Sam knew that this might qualify as the riskiest dare he had ever encountered. Self-preservation told him that he'd better back off. He took a deep breath and counted to ten.

"Are you ready?" he called over his shoulder.

"I'm all set," Tessa replied, her voice muffled.

"Then put your arms around my waist and hold on."

Tessa bit her lip. Put her arms around his waist? As if it wasn't bad enough to be pressed up against a back that felt like the Great Wall of China. Bad enough to be subjected to be the combined scents of leather, expensive cologne and Sam. Bad enough to have her legs wrapped around him in a way that sent x-rated thoughts careening through her mind. And she couldn't object. Not without letting Sam know how he affected her.

Tessa resisted the urge to trail her hands in a slow path

from his shoulders to his waist. Instead, she took a deep breath and gingerly encircled him with her arms.

"Tighter!" Sam snapped, his voice rough. "I don't want you flying off when I turn a corner."

"Then watch your speed."

Sam revved the engine once and the motorcycle moved forward.

"When I lean, you lean in the same direction," Sam called.

Suddenly Tessa didn't need any urging to hold on tight. It had been five years since she had been on a motorcycle and longer than that since she had been a passenger instead of the driver. She knew her vise-like grip must be uncomfortable, yet she couldn't bring herself to loosen it.

Sam leaned to the left and the motorcycle turned away from the flooded intersection. Tessa had no choice but to lean with him, swallowing a startled gasp as the motorcycle picked up speed. Somehow in the past few years she seemed to have lost her taste for adventure.

"Not so fast!" she called breathlessly.

"We're going twenty-five miles an hour," Sam yelled back. "Any slower and we might as well be pushing the damned thing."

Funny, Tessa thought, she would have sworn they were going at least sixty. She gritted her teeth, determined to get through the ride with no further comments.

By craning her neck, she was able to see over Sam's left shoulder and keep track of their progress. The breeze lifted the hair from her shoulders and rushed over her skin. Tessa squinted her eyes to keep dust from getting in her contacts and wished her helmet had a face guard like Sam's.

Suddenly she was enjoying the ride. And not just because she was hanging on to the best male body she had ever encountered, but because it was fun.

"You can go faster, if you want to." The words popped out before Tessa could stop them.

The motorcycle surged forward. Tessa didn't even try to stifle a whoop of exhilaration.

They sped down streets and around corners. Old reflexes kicked in and soon she was leaning into the turns with Sam.

They pulled into the Music Institute's parking lot, the scene of Flossie's accident. Tessa swallowed hard, trying to get rid of a sudden tightness in her throat.

"My car is over there."

Sam parked the cycle and killed the engine. Tessa slid off the back and walked toward a wood-paneled station wagon from the era when cars were built like battleships and gas was cheap.

Sam pictured his grandmother trapped under the wheel of this old tank. A wave of anger shook him. How could Tessa have been so careless?

Tessa stood next to the station wagon, fumbling in her purse and finally retrieving a set of keys. She bent down to unlock the door and froze. The keys clattered to the ground unnoticed as Tessa leaned over and picked something up.

Sam leaped off the motorcycle and ran over to Tessa, who was cradling a woman's shoe in her hands. Gran's shoe.

Tessa's face was ashen in the glare of the mercury vapor lamps. Sweat beaded her forehead and upper lip. Tears slid down her cheeks unnoticed. Her voice was a harsh whisper as she repeated the same words over and over.

"Oh, Flossie. Oh, Flossie. Oh, Flossie."

Sam made a quick decision. He picked up the keys and put his arm around Tessa.

"I'm driving you home," he said.

Chapter Three

Sam tried to figure out what had gone wrong. He was supposed to be driving Tessa home, not following her.

On the other hand, given Tessa's stubborn streak, he was lucky she had agreed to a compromise. If being told to go away and leave her alone could be considered a compromise.

Good Samaritans didn't get nearly enough credit, Sam reflected. It would have been so easy to take Tessa at her word and leave, but the doctor in him wouldn't allow it. Hell, neither would the man.

The doctor wanted to drag her back to the hospital and keep her under observation overnight to make sure she wasn't suffering from shock.

The man wanted to take her in his arms and reassure her that Flossie was going to be fine. Then he wanted to get her home, make sure she had something to eat, and massage the tension from her muscles until she fell asleep.

At which point, he acknowledged ruefully, he would be suffering a great deal of muscular tension himself.

The doctor hadn't gotten his way. Neither had the man. Tessa, however, had.

Which was why he was following her ancient station wagon into the driveway of a gray cottage. The headlights of Tessa's car swept past a riot of crimson roses that cascaded from the porch roof to the ground.

Sam parked his motorcycle and took a deep breath. The scent that perfumed the night air reminded him of Tessa's tantalizing fragrance. He loved it.

Tessa jumped out of the station wagon and hurried toward the house.

"Oh, no." Sam swung himself off the cycle and caught up with Tessa as she reached the front door. "I'm going to check you over and make sure you're settled for the night."

A flicker of light caught Sam's eye. He glanced over at it and did a double take. "Am I hallucinating?" he demanded. "Or is there really a fluorescent hand in your window?"

"There really is a fluorescent hand, and you really are hallucinating if you think you're going to do anything but say good night and leave."

"Tessa, if you weren't in shock back at the parking lot, you were damned close . . ." Sam paused and took another look at the ghostly blue outline. *"Why* is there a fluorescent hand in the window?" How the hell, he wondered, could this woman derail his train of thought so effortlessly? "Are you a palm reader in your spare time?"

"No," she replied, unlocking the lace curtained front door. "That was my grandmother. Although she really preferred tea leaves or tarot cards."

"She was a fortuneteller?" Sam asked incredulously.

"Right up to the day she died." Tessa paused in the doorway. "I'm tired, Sam. I'll tell you all about Grandmother some other time, but right now I want to take a nice hot bath, have a bite to eat, and go to bed.''

"Very good." Sam nudged Tessa gently into the house. "Just what the doctor was about to order."

"Well, then, drive carefully, say hi to Flossie if you see her before I do, thanks for following me home, and good night." Tessa rattled everything off in one breath and swung the door toward him.

Sam braced one hand against it. "Do you live alone?" He saw the wary look that sprang into her eyes and continued. "Because if you do, I'm not leaving until you're out of the tub."

"Want to bet?" Tessa raised her eyebrows in an unmistakable challenge and Sam knew she had him. He couldn't force his way into the house if she didn't want him there.

"Okay," Sam said. "How about this? I won't check you over, but I'll stay until you're ready for bed." He glanced at his watch. "Which shouldn't take very long. I'd say you can take a quick bath, eat, and be in bed in thirty minutes."

"Stop it!" Tessa slapped her hand against the door. "What if I want to soak in the tub for an hour? Suppose I'd like to eat first? Don't tell me what to do!" She heaved an exasperated sigh. "Good night, Dr. Caldwell."

"Please." Sam laid a finger across Tessa's lips before she could protest further. "If I go home now, I'll spend the rest of the night wondering if you fell asleep in the tub and drowned."

Her lips were soft under his finger and he had to resist an almost overwhelming desire to rub the finger back and forth across the satiny flesh. Something in Tessa's startled gaze told Sam that she might not mind if he did.

"Well," Tessa finally murmured, her breath hot against his skin. "I wouldn't want to be responsible for a sleepless night." She opened the door wider and gestured for him to enter.

Sam hesitated, every instinct telling him to leave if he valued his peace of mind. Sleepless night? Hell, he'd probably be awake for the next week, trying to relive every sensation this exasperating, fascinating woman aroused in him.

"Thank you." Sam stepped inside and was greeted by a menacing growl.

"Quiet, Ruzsi!" Tessa snapped on a light and Sam saw a large grey dog standing with one paw barely touching the polished oak floor of the hallway on the other side of the living room. Its other three paws were planted firmly on the living room rug, an exquisite oriental. The animal's pale grey eyes regarded him steadily. And, Sam thought, a bit dubiously.

"Oh, Ruzsi, you know you're not allowed in here. One foot in the hall doesn't count." Tessa snapped her fingers and pointed to the hall. The dog backed up and sat at attention.

"Roozhee?" Sam tried to duplicate Tessa's pronunciation.

"Hungarian for Rosie."

"What made you call her that?"

Tessa gave Sam a baffled glance. "I like the name. What would you have picked?"

Sam glanced over at the dog's sleek grey coat and startling pale eyes. "Shadow, maybe. Or Smoky. Something that relates to the animal's appearance or temperament."

Tessa rolled her eyes and walked over to the dog. "This is Sam, Ruzsi. Also known as Mr. Literal."

"Dr. Literal to you." Sam took Ruzsi's outstretched paw and scratched her ears with his free hand. "You talk to the dog?"

"Of course," Tessa said brightly, "she's my best friend, aren't you, girl?"

The dog's tail beat a brisk tattoo on the oak floor, as if, Sam thought, the animal understood Tessa's words.

Tessa laughed. "Dr. Caldwell thinks we're crazy, Ruzsi." Her eyes twinkled at him. "Don't you, Sam?"

"I think you should get some rest." And if that wasn't a slick evasion, Sam thought, he'd eat his stethoscope.

"You're right." Tessa sat down on the bottom step of a staircase in the hallway. "As long as you've conned your way into my house," she said, unbuckling her shoes, "you might as well make yourself useful. So while I'm in the tub, you can make us a pot of chamomile tea and something to eat. There's coffee, too, if you're not into herbal tea." She stood up, her frivolous pink shoes dangling from one hand.

"Okay," Sam shrugged. "If your security guard lets me."

Tessa chuckled. "Now that I've introduced you to Ruzsi, she'll be fine."

Sam glanced down at Ruzsi, whose steely gaze reminded him of a judge about to sentence a repeat offender. "How reassuring."

"The kitchen is through the swinging door. Leftovers and sandwich stuff are in the refrigerator, so go wild and create anything you like. Meanwhile, I'll hop in the tub." Tessa yawned and clasped her arms over her head in a long stretch that emphasized every curve.

Sam turned away abruptly. There was just so much temptation a good Samaritan could take. "Fine. And if you're not down here in twenty minutes, Ruzsi and I will come looking for you."

He didn't wait for a reply, but pushed the swinging door and went into the kitchen. The dog followed at his heels.

Once inside, Sam almost jumped back into the hall, assaulted by a riot of color and clutter. He squinted, waited a moment, and opened his eyes cautiously. He wasn't dreaming.

Another large oriental rug covered much of the kitchen floor. Worn in spots, the rug still glowed like scattered jewels on the faded red linoleum. Centered on the rug was a heavy oak table piled high with books, magazines, and mail. Four wooden stools were pulled up to it. Ruzsi left Sam's side and settled under the table with a contented sigh.

Relieved to be rid of his canine chaperon, Sam tossed his leather jacket on a stool and walked around the table to the other side of the kitchen. A traditional breakfast nook area had been turned into something that could have been a greenhouse, a photo gallery, a small sitting room, or all of them.

Two white wicker chairs, one a rocker, sat on either side of a glass-topped table. Ivy and ferns curtained the large windows. Scarlet geraniums on the sills added an unnecessary touch of color to the kaleidoscopic room.

"Good God, Ruzsi, how can she live with all this . . . stuff?" He looked at the dog and sighed. "I'm talking to you, too. This house must be a breeding ground for eccentric behavior and I'm coming down with the virus."

Ruzsi thumped her tail on the rug and smiled. Sam knew intellectually that it was only a reflexive lifting of the muzzle, but it certainly resembled a toothy grin.

As his mind began to deal with the sensory overload, Sam could see that the room had a certain peculiar order to it. A gleaming copper kettle stood on a vintage gas stove that was just as spotless. Ceramic and glass containers of various shapes were ranged on the counters, each bearing a neatly printed label.

Looking as if it had been transported from the psychedelic '60's, the refrigerator stood in bold contrast to the stove. Most of its white enamel surface was covered with vividly colored drawings, jokes, and quotations, each one signed by a different person. Sam scanned the various contributions, smiling at some, pausing thoughtfully over others, noticing a number of names from the hospital staff.

A rainbow of washable markers stood in a coffee mug

on the counter and a note invited guests to add their handiwork to the "art show." Sam rejected the notion without a second thought.

He filled the kettle, set it on the stove to boil, and opened the refrigerator door. This time he half expected what he was going to find. Cartons of whole milk and heavy cream. Several pounds of butter. A pint of sour cream. An assortment of jams, jellies, pickles, relishes, and dressings that would have done credit to a gourmet specialty shop.

Covered casseroles held leftovers. Sam recognized roast pork with sauerkraut and caraway. Another held spaetzles. He suspected the third one contained goulash. The meat drawer yielded goose liver and enough cheese to keep a family of mice with eclectic tastes content for weeks.

The whole refrigerator was a classic example of dietary folly. Anyone who ate like that was a cardiac time bomb.

Only the crisper drawers and a loaf of whole wheat bread gave Sam any hope of putting together a suitable meal for Tessa. He decided on fresh fruit, toast with strawberry jam, and chamomile tea. The jam wasn't sugar free, but it was as close to a nutritious snack as he could get.

The kettle's piercing whistle reminded Sam of the tea. He pulled a couple of tea bags from the proper jar, put them in the pot and poured boiling water over them.

He assembled a tray and looked around, considering. Reading glasses rested on a stack of books next to the rocker, indicating that Tessa often sat there.

As he set the tray on the table between the wicker chairs, the wall of photographs caught his eye.

Most appeared to be family pictures that went back many years. There was even a wedding tintype of a stern looking man with a handlebar mustache standing protectively next to a woman who bore a strong resemblance to Tessa. Was this the fortune telling grandmother?

His interest captured, Sam searched the wall for pictures

of Tessa as a little girl. They weren't easy to find. Like everything else in the room, the photographs appeared to be in no particular order, but Sam was sure that Tessa had a reason, however illogical, for the way they were arranged.

She had been a beautiful child. Sam chuckled at a picture of Tessa peering over a beach ball almost as big as she was. The camera caught the same laughing expression in her eyes that had captivated Sam when she was talking to Flossie.

He spotted pictures of Tessa in school plays, rolling in autumn leaves, smiling up at a gangly young basketball player.

Straightening from inspecting a Halloween picture of Tessa in Gypsy garb, Sam glanced around to see if he had missed anything. A photograph near the ceiling caught his eye and he took it down for a closer look.

It was Tessa and four young men, arms linked together, hamming it up for the camera. All of them wore leather and had hair that hung well below their shoulders. Sam unconsciously ran a hand over his own sensible cut as he scrutinized the picture. Something about Tessa nagged at his subconscious, but he couldn't pinpoint what it was.

In the photo, Tessa's hair curled down to her waist in wild disarray. Her leather pants looked as if they been surgically attached to her body. A fringed and studded leather vest barely covered a black lace bodysuit that hugged her curves like a Ferrari in a road race. Earrings made of silver disks and colorful stones shimmered almost to her shoulders and a silver chain around her neck bore a single large crystal that nestled between her breasts. Her wide grey eyes twinkled at the camera through a tangle of false lashes and her full lips, coated with something that made them look like dew-touched cherries, were parted in an exaggerated movie star pout.

Sam sucked in his breath and let it out in a whoosh,

more aroused by the image than he wanted to admit to himself.

"Damn it," he muttered, "where have I seen you before?"

"In the hallway, about twenty minutes ago."

Sam turned and saw Tessa coming through the kitchen door. He glanced down at the picture in his hand and back at Tessa.

Except for a few damp strands clinging to the nape of her neck, Tessa's hair was hidden by a towel. Her face was scrubbed and shiny.

Dr. Caldwell was pleased to see that her cheeks and lips were a healthy pink, a nice contrast to the pallor that had worried him in the parking lot.

Sam Caldwell barely registered such mundane medical details. He wanted to stroke her glowing skin, to find out first hand if the creamy texture was as soft as it appeared. He wanted to kiss that generous mouth, to feel her rosy lips yield under his, promising further delights. He wanted to pull the towel from her hair and let his fingers comb through the luxuriant mass.

Sam's gaze wandered down to Tessa's robe, a worn white garment that reminded him of an old-fashioned bedspread. He swallowed hard. Tessa in bedspread material was more seductive than most women in satin.

Her unconfined breasts shifted entrancingly under the fabric with every breath she took. The robe tied at her waist and flared out again over deliciously curved hips, stopping just above her ankles.

Sam stared at Tessa's feet. Two pink pig slippers stared back at him.

"Holy Cow!" Sam said. "Or should I say, Holy Sow!" He looked down at the photo in his hand. "I see you've changed designers."

Tessa made an exasperated sound and reached for the picture.

"Uh-uh." He whisked it out of reach. "Not until I'm through looking at it."

"Suit yourself." Tessa shrugged with elaborate nonchalance. After glancing at the tray Sam had prepared, she headed toward the refrigerator.

"This looks so familiar and I can't imagine why. Where would I have seen these guys?"

Tessa gave him a peculiar look. "Most likely at a concert." She took two casseroles from the refrigerator and spooned goulash and spaetzles on a plate. "On MTV, if you watch it." She popped the plate into the microwave and punched the keypads.

"MTV?" Sam asked absently, frowning at the picture. He glanced over at Tessa, too focused on the mystery of the picture to wonder at the incredulous look on her face. "This is going to drive me nuts until I remember." He slumped down in one of the wicker chairs. "Come on, don't torture me. Who are these four guys? Where was the picture taken?"

Tessa leaned against the counter and sipped her tea. "The four guys founded *Uprising* and the picture was taken backstage."

Sam glanced again at the picture and hazarded a guess. "A singing group?"

"No, Sam, political activists." Tessa's sarcastic reply told Sam he had blundered.

"Oh, sure, *Uprising*." Sam wondered how he could pry more information out of her without wounding her feelings again. "That's the group that . . ." He snapped his fingers as if trying to jog his memory.

". . . caused the riot." Tessa gave a brittle laugh. "The group whose concert turned into a disaster when there weren't enough security people to handle a fight. The group that has to remember that twenty people left the concert in ambulances. The group that has to live with the knowledge that one of those people will never walk again."

"And you were there?"

"You could say that." Tessa closed her eyes and shuddered breath. "I was *Uprising*'s lead singer." She opened her eyes and gave him a somber look. "The one who was pulled off the stage into the mob."

Chapter Four

Sam's apologetic shrug told Tessa that incredibly, he didn't remember the event that had shattered her life five years ago.

"Curiosity satisfied?" Tessa snatched the picture from Sam, climbed on the wicker chair, and replaced the photo on its hook.

"Uh-uh." Sam shook his head. "Not until I hear the rest of the story. Did you get hurt?"

"Yes." The microwave beeped and Tessa removed the goulash, looked at it with sudden distaste and set it on the counter.

"How bad?"

Sam's voice was so unexpectedly gentle that Tessa almost burst into tears. Instead she pulled the towel from her hair, bent over, and started shaking out the tangles so she wouldn't have to look at the unsettling sympathy in his eyes.

"A broken arm and neon bruises. Not nearly as painful

as the guilt, though. For months I kept telling myself that there must have been something I could have done." Tessa straightened up and flipped her hair back. "Dumb, huh."

Sam nodded in agreement. "Real dumb. Just the kind of thing I've done myself when a mission didn't go perfectly."

Tessa gave Sam a lopsided grin. "Knowing that I've ever shared a thought with you is pretty terrifying."

"I'll bet."

Sam grinned back and Tessa's pulse quickened, just as it had in the emergency room. How could a simple smile cause such change? The craggy hollows in Sam's face became laugh lines and the icy depths of his eyes warmed to the color of tropic lagoons, inviting Tessa to lose herself in them. The chiseled line of his mouth relaxed into a barely resistible temptation.

Uninvited visions danced through her mind: Sam leaning toward her, his eyes beckoning, promising, his mouth brushing hers in a kiss so soft, so tantalizing that Tessa's lips parted involuntarily, eager for more. . . .

"So," Sam continued. "Was that the end of *Uprising*?"

Tessa blinked twice, snapped her mouth shut and attempted to collect her scattered wits. "The end?"

"Well, apparently you're not singing with them these days, so I assumed that the group folded. And if they didn't, why aren't you still with them?"

"Hard to say." *Impossible, in fact, to explain the fear that gripped her at the thought of performing in front of a live audience again, a terror so overwhelming that she couldn't even sing in the relative privacy of the recording studio.*

"I felt like a change, I guess." *Especially when faced with the prospect of holding the group back while she attempted to work out her problems in therapy.*

"So I left." *How much heartache, how many tears were summed up in those three words!*

"As for the group," she continued, "the concert from

hell got so much publicity that they had to hire somebody to sort out the record offers and requests for concert dates."

Because the band was left without a manager after the police arrested her fiancé. Fraud, embezzlement—the list of charges went on and on. The awful truth that she had been engaged to this man still made Tessa question her ability to judge character.

Sam looked puzzled. "I don't get it. Why would a disastrous concert have such a positive impact?"

"You know the old saying—any publicity is better than no publicity. That's what gave the group the final push from opening for the superstar groups to being one."

"And yet you left when they were on the edge of real success." Sam nodded his head thoughtfully. "I wonder if residual emotional trauma might have been an unconscious factor in your decision to leave the group."

Tessa's mouth went dry and she mentally cursed Sam Caldwell's unerring diagnostic instincts. She didn't answer for a moment. Part of her longed to tell him everything, but part urged caution. If he knew all about her failed relationship with Don and her inability to conquer her fear of performing, Sam might decide that she was a poor judge of character and emotionally unstable. Not an image that would improve Sam's view of music therapists. She couldn't take that risk—not before the appropriations committee meeting.

Tessa shrugged casually. "Oh, I don't think so." She wasn't lying, she reminded herself. *There had been nothing unconscious about her decision.*

"Are they still performing?"

Tessa laughed incredulously. "You don't know that they kicked off their second world tour two weeks ago?"

"I'm not interested in music," Sam explained. "So why would I know?"

"Because they're one of the top bands in the world! Everyone knows them!"

Sam shook his head. "Wrong. I don't."

"That's just incredible." She looked at Sam doubtfully, trying to decide if he was teasing her.

"Why?"

"Because ... because ...," Tessa sputtered. "How can you keep up with current events and not know about *Uprising?*" she finished in a rush.

"Hmm." Sam pondered her question. "You're saying that there are certain things any intelligent person knows, right?"

Tessa mulled over Sam's question, sure that she was being led into a trap. "Yes," she agreed hesitantly.

"Who won the Super Bowl last year?" The wicked gleam in Sam's eyes said "Gotcha!"

Tessa did a rapid scan of her mental memory-banks and came up empty. "That's easy," she bluffed. "A football team."

Sam shook his head. "Uh-uh. Generalities won't do."

"The name slips my mind," Tessa said with as much dignity as she could muster. "That doesn't prove anything."

"It doesn't?" Sam's bushy eyebrows lifted skeptically. "Tell me the name of the Secretary of Defense. What book is number one on the *New York Times* best seller list? Who is the current Miss America?"

"As if you know about Miss America!"

"Yeah, but we've already established that I'm not up on current events. Shall we continue the quiz?"

"No!" Laughing, Tessa covered her ears and sank into the chair next to Sam. "You've made your point."

"Which is?"

"That I'm not as smart as I think I am."

"Nope." Sam shook him head. "The point is that you

expect everybody to look at things from your perspective, an illogical expectation at best and damned conceited at worst. You sang with a rock band, so everyone should recognize the name of that band."

Ignoring Tessa's outraged gasp, he continued. "Your position on reducing the music therapy appropriation is a perfect example. Take an objective look at the number of patients serviced by your department and the cost of running it. You'll have to admit the figures don't make sense. If you spent the same amount of money on diagnostic equipment, at least twice as many patients would benefit."

Sam's voice was lazy, almost reflective, yet his words ignited Tessa's temper like a match in dry tinder. Leaping to her feet, she shoved her hands deep into the pockets of her chenille robe and battled the urge to shake him until she rattled some compassion into his analytical, bottom line, let's-look-at-the-figures brain.

"You're confusing a hospital with a gas station, Dr. Caldwell. We don't service patients, we help them. *Help* them. We treat them like people, Dr. Caldwell, not numbers. Do you have any idea what kinds of patients the music therapy department worked with last year? Do you, Dr. Caldwell? Try looking at individuals instead of the bottom line for once. You'll be amazed at how different things appear, Dr. Caldwell."

"Sam." Only one laconic word, but the icy glint in Sam's eyes and the muscle twitching along his jaw told Tessa that she had lit Sam's notoriously short fuse.

"And no matter how different things may appear from a music therapist's viewpoint, I'm a surgeon and I know this much: you can't cure a patient without an accurate diagnosis. You *can* cure a patient without music therapy."

"True." Tessa nodded her agreement. "You can also perform surgery without anesthesia, but it's easier with it."

"Oh, come on!" Sam jumped up and stood facing her, not even trying to disguise his irritation. "How can you compare music therapy with anesthesia?"

"They both relieve pain," Tessa answered quietly.

Sam made a strangled noise. "That's ridiculous. Anesthesia is a measurable, controllable procedure that has predictable results. Can you say the same about music therapy?"

"Don't you *dare* call my profession ridiculous!" Tessa punctuated each word by jabbing Sam's chest with her forefinger.

"I didn't! I merely pointed out the illogic of comparing an anatomically explainable procedure with something as elusive as the effect of music on the healing process."

"Why am I explaining things to you?" Tessa threw her hands up in a gesture of resignation. "You're just like Don—if the numbers are right, nothing else matters."

"Don who?" Sam glared at Tessa.

"*Uprising*'s former manager." Her lips tightened and her voice was harsh. "Another person who made decisions without weighing their impact on people."

"And don't *you* dare imply that the patients' best interests aren't my first priority."

Sam's eyebrows drew together and his face darkened in a way that would have sent most hospital personnel scurrying in the opposite direction. Tessa remained unfazed.

"I wasn't," she replied coolly. "I was merely pointing out that newer disciplines have a legitimate place in the medical hierarchy, a fact you conveniently ignore."

"There you go again!" Sam exclaimed. "You think that music therapy should be funded no matter what else has to be eliminated, so anyone who doesn't agree is not only wrong, but insensitive to boot. What an ego!"

"I don't have to listen to this." Tessa turned away

abruptly. "Good night. I'm going to bed." She started toward the hallway.

"Well, at least you're consistent." Sam's hand shot out and circled Tessa's wrist. "It's a tough situation, so you're running away."

A low growl told Sam that Ruzsi didn't much care for his behavior, while the expression on Tessa's face suggested that he'd be better off dealing with the dog than with her.

"Meaning?" Tessa tried to pull her hand away, but Sam wouldn't let go.

"You left that singing group rather than work through your problems and now you're ducking a controversy with me."

Tessa yanked her hand harder this time, but San tightened his grasp until his fingers met around her wrist. Damn, but she was strong for her size!

Behind him, Ruzsi turned up the volume on the growl and flashed Sam a glimpse of business-like teeth.

"Sit and be quiet, Ruzsi! I'll fight my own battles, thank you." Tessa waited while the dog slowly complied and then turned her flinty gaze toward Sam.

"Let go of my arm. Now."

Under the smooth skin of her forearm, Tessa's muscles were taut and quivering, whether from anger or fatigue, Sam couldn't decide. It certainly wasn't desire, he reflected wryly, and suddenly wished it was. He could imagine all too vividly those slender arms twined around his neck, pulling his head down to hers for a kiss. Not that she'd have to exert much pressure.

Sam's gaze settled on Tessa's mouth. Even the angry set of her jaw couldn't detract from those luscious lips, pale pink now without lipstick, but still as full and moist as they had appeared in the group picture. He fought the urge to kiss her, knowing that if Ruzsi didn't bite him, Tessa probably would.

Sucking in a deep breath, Sam released Tessa's arm, berating himself for ending the evening on such an unpleasant note, sure that she would bolt for the door.

But she didn't. Instead Tessa wrapped her arms tightly around herself, as if trying to give herself a reassuring hug and stared at him, the anger muted by hurt.

"Why?" Tessa asked. "Why would you say something so unkind?"

Sam looked away from her accusing gaze, rubbed the back of his neck and finally shrugged. "My background is combat and rescue, not communication. I say what I think and it gets me into trouble sometimes."

"I know," Tessa said. "I work at the hospital, remember?"

Sam nodded ruefully. "I guess you've seen me in action."

"Once or twice. But you still haven't answered my question. It was what you meant, not how you said it that hurt." Tessa paused. "Although it could have been phrased more diplomatically. Do you really think I was running away from something tonight? Or any other time?"

"Let's drop it, Tessa. It's late, you're tired, and you still haven't eaten anything. I'll clear out and let you have some peace." Sam took a marker from the coffee mug and sketched a stick figure dangling from a parachute in a blank corner of the refrigerator door.

"Now who's running away?" Tessa arched one eyebrow. "I'm too wound up to sleep right now, so I'm going to take that plate of fruit and the chamomile tea outside and have a middle of the night picnic with Ruzsi. You can do whatever you want."

She gathered the mug and plate, clutching them in one

hand while she unlocked the back door and held it open for Ruzsi. The pair disappeared into the blackness outside.

Sam stood frowning at the picture he had just drawn. So far his efforts at changing Tessa's mind about the hospital budget were on a par with his artistic effort: pathetic.

Sam sighed, picked up his leather jacket from the stool, slung it over his shoulder, and headed for the door. Giving the swinging door a vigorous shove, he paused and let the door fall back against his outstretched hand. Damned if he'd let her think he was running away from her!

Retracing his footsteps, Sam threw his jacket on the stool again, picked up his tea from the counter, and marched through the back door.

Sam stood on the steps and waited for his eyes to adjust to the darkness, once again surrounded by the overpowering scent of the roses that climbed over every available space.

Peering into the yard, he saw a giant oak tree that obscured a large patch of the star-studded sky. A rhythmic creaking was the only sound that broke the quiet of the night.

He walked cautiously toward the tree, uncertain of Ruzsi's whereabouts. As he approached the oak, Sam saw a wooden porch swing hanging from a massive limb. Tessa was seated on it, apparently absorbed in the starlight filtering through the branches. The collar of her white robe was pulled up against the cool night air. Her porcine footwear alternately turned reproachful eyes toward him and dug their snouts into the damp grass as Tessa pushed the swing back and forth.

On the ground next to the swing sat the fruit and tea. Nearby, two pale eyes flicked between Tessa and the food, the only sign that Ruzsi was lying there.

Sam cleared his throat. "Will it hold two people?"

"There's only one way to find out." Tessa shifted toward the end of the swing and Sam sat down. The limb creaked, dipped slightly, and then settled in its new position. Sam and Tessa rocked together in a silence that was far from comfortable.

After considering and discarding several conversational gambits, he spoke.

"I was way out of line tonight."

"You sure were."

Tessa's unexpected agreement made Sam laugh abruptly.

"You didn't pull any punches, either," he reminded Tessa.

"Just following your lead, Doctor." Her voice was tranquil, almost remote as she continued searching the night sky through the lacy pattern of the branches.

"Still mad?"

Tessa shook her head. "Still waiting to hear why you said I was running away again."

"Forget it, okay? I already admitted I was wrong." Sam leaned back and laced his fingers behind his head. "Why waste time arguing when we could be enjoying the stars and the night breeze and the quiet?" He braced his feet against the ground to stop the motion of the swing and peered up through the branches. "Look," he said, "there's Casseopeia."

"I'm surprised," Tessa said, curling her legs up on the swing. Two sideway pig faces stared impassively at Sam. He fought the urge to pull the hem of her robe over them.

"Surprised about what? That I recognize a constellation?" Sam laughed. "That's one of the first things you learn in the Air Force. After all, if you're going to be flying around up there, it helps to know the road signs."

"Ha!" Tessa exclaimed with satisfaction. "Just as I thought. You look at a spectacular night sky and see road signs. Not much of a nature lover, are you!"

"If I wasn't, why would I enjoy white water rafting and

extreme skiing so much?" Sam caught her quizzical glance and continued. "Extreme skiing involves trekking or taking a helicopter into an area where you'll find very few, if any other skiers."

"My guess," said Tessa, a chuckle warming her voice, "is that you enjoy those things because they're difficult, dangerous and they make you feel macho as hell."

"Yeah," Sam conceded with a laugh. "You're right on all counts. But those aren't the only, or even the most important reasons." He hitched one leg up on the swing and turned to face Tessa, eager to make her understand.

"When you're all alone, thousands of feet up on a mountain, it's like you own the place, Tessa. All that vastness, all that perfection—the sun, the air, the pristine snow . . . It's the most awesome damned feeling in the world, like you're king of the mountain and yet so small and insignificant. Even pictures only hint at the beauty. They can't capture the clean smell or the stillness or the way the wind chills you and the sun warms you, all at the same time." Sam spread his hands in frustration "I'm not much good with words," he said.

"You're good enough to make me wish I could see it."

"Why not?" Sam asked. "Don't you ski?"

Tessa laughed. "No, Sam, I don't ski. My grandmother raised me on a widow's pension. It doesn't go far, even supplemented by a little fortune-telling on the side. Skiing's not cheap, so my winter sports were limited to building snow forts and fighting snowball battles."

"It's never too late to start." Sam said.

"True, but I'm not like you, Sam. I'm me, and somehow I'm contented with quieter adventures."

The night breeze freshened and blew a strand of hair against her lips. Sam and Tessa reached simultaneously to free it, and their hands met and held.

Sam moved a little closer to Tessa, and linked his fingers

more securely through hers, unwilling to break the contact between them. Once again, he could feel a fine tremor in her hand, but this time, he was almost certain it was for a different reason. Even in the dim light, Tessa's gaze was luminous.

"You might find you have a taste for adventure if you give it a chance." His other hand gently stroked her face and he heard Tessa take a deep breath and hold it.

Her lips were parted, eager. Sam battled the urge to taste those lips and did something he had never done in his life: surrendered with only token resistance. He leaned closer until the space between them could be measured in inches. His hand slid under her hair and cupped the back of her neck, caressing the soft down he found there.

Tessa's eyes widened, and then closed. Her warm breath caressed his lips a moment before they touched hers.

It was a soft kiss, a gentle kiss, a kiss didn't even rate a glance from Ruzsi, yet it set off the physiological equivalent of fireworks in Sam's body.

Time stood still. Time rushed by. Sam wasn't sure which. He only knew that he wasn't the one who pulled back.

Tessa stared up at him, her eyes wide, sending him conflicting messages. Please stop. Please don't stop.

"It's just a kiss," he said, lying through his teeth. "A friendly kiss between two people who've had a tough day. See?" He dipped his head and took her lips, savoring the sweet taste of her, the silken touch of her, the simmering warmth of her.

Tessa's lips softened and parted under his for a moment, but then she pulled away. "I can't do this," she said breathlessly.

"Why not?" Sam asked, baffled. He knew that his body wouldn't be reacting the way it was without encouragement.

"I can't explain, either." Tessa slid her feet to the ground and tried to stand up, but Sam tugged her back.

"Let's talk, Tessa. It's always better to confront things than run away."

Even as he spoke, Sam knew he had committed a strategic error. He could almost picture the sentence coming out of his mouth, as if he was a cartoon character and there was a big white bubble over his head with the inflammatory words in bold print.

Any faint hopes that Tessa had missed his blunder were scorched and turned to ashes under the look she directed at him. "Did it ever occur to you," she demanded, "that maybe I don't like kissing you?"

"No," Sam replied honestly. "Because it's not true. You *loved* kissing me, at least for the first few minutes."

Tessa leaped to her feet and the swing rocked wildly in protest. "Your ego wouldn't fit on Mt. Rushmore!"

"What surgeon's would?" Sam gave her a wry grin. "But the point is that I kissed you and you kissed me back."

Tessa tossed her hair and shrugged. "Just a brief physical reaction. Big deal."

"Yeah," Sam agreed, "it was a big deal, and then suddenly it wasn't. And when I tried to find out why . . ." He spread his hands in a gesture of frustration.

"Okay," Tessa said wearily. "Let's get this over with. You're evidently going to keep harping on this running away thing until you speak your piece, so go to it!" She plopped back down on the swing, well away from Sam, and folded her arms.

Sam heaved a frustrated sigh. "I'm baffled, Tessa. You and the other members of *Uprising* must have worked like hell to get your shot at the big time. And when the chance came along, you tossed it away! Not just your own chance, but the group's as well. How long did it take to find a singer to take your place?"

"They didn't look for one," Tessa said. "Gavin—*Uprising*'s leader—thought it would be good for the band to go in a little different direction after what had happened."

"Would he have thought that if you hadn't forced his hand?"

Tessa pulled her feet up on the swing and hugged her knees to her chest. "Why is a guy who doesn't like music so interested in me and my former career?" She tilted a glance at him. "Most surgeons act as if feelings and emotions don't exist, yet you've spent the evening doing Sigmund Freud impressions with me. Why?"

Sam raked a hand through his hair, trying to find a way to sugar coat the truth and failing.

"Because," he said, "you've launched a campaign for your department that would do credit to a seasoned general. You seem like a real fighter, full of dogged determination, and I respect that, even though I don't share your viewpoint." Sam hesitated, took a deep breath, and went on. "But there's the thing with the band. Based on the way you're handling the appropriations committee, I would have expected you to tackle whatever problems you had with the group and solve them, but you quit instead."

Tessa lifted her head and tried to speak, but Sam held up one hand and hurried on.

"I know, I know, you think I don't understand your situation, but I do. Since that accident sidelined me from the Air Force Reserves, I've had to confront long odds and dismal medical predictions, but I'm determined to get back to my Pararescue unit. Sometimes I get discouraged, but I keep on working toward the goal. And my own experience makes me wonder why you didn't fight harder for your singing career."

"Probably because I have no desire to be Peter Pan." Tessa's voice was silky-soft, yet Sam's internal radar started picking up storm signals. "You know," Tessa continued, "the character who wouldn't grow up. Somehow that role never appealed to me. It doesn't to most women," she added thoughtfully. "We seem better equipped than men to face reality and move on to the next phase of our lives." She reached over and gave Sam's hand a maternal pat. The moon emerged from the clouds, revealing a gleam in Tessa's eyes that made Sam's internal radar issue a take cover alert. He ignored it.

"You're comparing me to Peter Pan."

Tessa's if-the-shoe-fits-wear-it shrug was a silent but eloquent answer.

Sam shook his head in disbelief. Tessa's distorted interpretation of his actions was so ludicrous that he wanted to chuckle. He wanted to poke holes in Tessa's ridiculous theory with a few pithy sentences. He wanted to explain the distinct difference between refusing to face reality and refusing to accept defeat. Most of all, he wanted to shake some common sense into her illogical, whimsical, never-mind-the-facts brain.

Remembering that the best defense isn't always a strong offense, Sam ignored all those tempting alternatives and summoned up an amiable smile. "You may be right, but that's unimportant. I still need to know who is the real Tessa Marcovy—the fighter or the quitter."

"I'm *not* a quitter." Tessa's satin voice was sounding a bit frayed. "And if I am, it's none of your business."

"True." Tessa gave him a startled glance. "As Sam Caldwell, the guy my grandmother is trying to get you to date, I don't much care. But as Dr. Caldwell, a member of the Appropriations Committee, it is very much my business."

Sam leaned forward and put a hand under her chin, tilting it so he could look into her eyes. "What if you get the funds to expand the Music Therapy department? Will you stick around to see it through? Or will you suddenly

quit and force us to suspend the project while we look for
another music therapist?''

Tessa slapped his hand away. "How many times do I
have to tell you? I didn't quit the band. I made a rational
choice after carefully evaluating my life and my goals.''

"What if your goals change again?''

"What if, what if, what if!'' Tessa sprang to her feet and
threw her hands in the air. "What if a meteor strikes the
hospital? What if a new ice age freezes North America into
a giant ice cube? What if there's a medical breakthrough
and surgeons become as obsolete as leeches? You could
imagine all kinds of improbable scenarios, Sam.''

"True, but this one has historical precedent. Maybe
there's some perfectly logical explanation . . .''

"There is!'' Tessa interjected. "I already told you.''

"Uh-uh.'' Sam shook his head. "I mean the underlying
reason, the thing that made you decide to evaluate your
life at that particular time.''

Tessa clenched and unclenched her hands several times,
opened her mouth to speak and shut it again, shaking her
head.

"Come on,'' Sam said gently. He stood up and put his
hands on her shoulders. Tessa looked up at him, her eyes
wary, her teeth worrying her bottom lip. "Whatever it is,
it can't possibly be as bad as you're imagining.''

A wry smile flickered across her lips. "Don't be so sure,''
she said.

Sam rubbed his thumbs along the base of her neck and
waited.

"After the disaster at the concert,'' she began slowly.

A high pitched sound made Tessa jump and Sam mutter
an earthy monosyllable. He pulled a pager from his pocket
and stepped from the tree's shadow into the moonlight.
Squinting, he looked at the pager and cursed again.

"It's the hospital, damn it!'' Sam stuffed the pager back

into his pocket and ground the heels of his hands into his tired eyes. "This better not be a motorcycle accident," he growled, heading for the house. "That's all I need, hours and hours of picking grass and gravel out of some speed demon's broken leg."

Sam's voice trailed off as he took the back steps two at a time and flung the door open.

" 'Some speed demon.' " Tessa grinned in spite of herself. "Talk about the pot calling the kettle black!" She picked up the dish from the grass and snapped her fingers for Ruzsi to follow.

The back door slapped against the wall and Sam ran down the steps toward Tessa.

"That was Flossie's doctor." Sam's voice was tight with worry. "He thinks she's developed a blood clot in her brain and wants to get her into surgery right away, but she won't go until she sees both of us."

Chapter Five

Tessa stared at the mangled coffee stirrer she'd been chewing, sighed, and added it to the steadily growing heap on the end table next to her. Glancing at her watch, she tapped it with her finger, hoping to see the numbers leap forward. Surely more than ten minutes had passed since the last time she checked.

Tessa looked around the empty waiting room. After three lonely hours, she would have settled for any form of human companionship. A young mother with endless pictures of precocious offspring—a football fan reeling off meaningless statistics—an earnest disciple of some fringe religious group hoping to steer her soul onto the One True Path—Tessa would have welcomed any or all of them. Even one of the officious volunteers who manned the waiting room desk during the day, dispensing platitudes and coffee, would have been a comfort.

She jumped up and paced over to the window. Her reflection stared back at her, eyes smudged with dark circles. Why wouldn't her body give in and let her sleep through this endless wait? Probably because too many cups of sugar-laced coffee had brought her soaring to a monumental caffeine/sugar high.

And now she was left simmering with restless energy that kept her tapping her fingers, shredding cardboard inserts from the vintage magazines, and creating towering pyramids of Styrofoam coffee cups.

Tessa braced her clenched fists on the marble sill and leaned her forehead against the cool windowpane.

Her heart ached for Sam. Flossie had begged him to be with her during the surgery, even though he couldn't take an active part, and Sam had promised. Tessa could only imagine how difficult the passive role of observer must be for Sam, whose admirers called him a take-charge sort of guy and whose detractors sourly referred to him as a control freak.

Tessa pushed herself away from the window and turned back to the waiting room. Still empty. She glanced up at the ceiling mounted TV. Still doing its imitation of a blizzard. She checked the coffee maker. Still some left in the pot. She shuddered and hastily averted her eyes.

She considered going down to her office and catching up on the eternal paperwork, but then clicked her tongue in exasperation. Sam had driven back to the hospital and had forgotten to give her the keys. And besides, she wouldn't be able to concentrate on anything but Sam and Flossie anyway.

Tessa gave up and plopped back down on the couch. Leaning forward, she propped her elbows on her thighs and pressed the heels of her hands against her eyes, trying not so much to relieve their gritty ache as to blot out the recurring memory of Flossie pinned under the station wagon.

Bad enough that she had broken Flossie's ankle, but to

have caused brain damage as well was another story. Would Flossie's impish personality be changed? Would she be able to speak? To read? To take care of herself? The questions were endless, the answers uncertain.

A light touch on her shoulder brought Tessa's head up, and her startled gaze met Sam's weary eyes.

"Gran's fine," he said, answering the question that was hovering on Tessa's lips. "Move over."

Tessa hastily obeyed and Sam sprawled next to her on the couch, groaning. He closed his eyes, folded his arms behind his head, stretched his legs out, and kicked off his shoes, still encased in paper surgical boots.

Tessa sat on the edge of the couch, waiting for Sam to continue. Seconds lengthened into minutes until Tessa couldn't stand the suspense.

"Well?"

One eyelid opened half-way and Sam peered at her. "Well, what? I told you, Gran's fine." His eyelid drifted down.

"What do you mean by fine? Fine, she survived the surgery or fine, she'll recovery completely?" Tessa grabbed his arm. "Come on, Sam, give me some details. I've been waiting out here forever and I want to know exactly what was wrong and how they fixed it and if Flossie will ever be back to normal."

"Oh, that's right, you don't know." He opened both eyes and looked up at her. "The leaky vessel in Gran's brain had nothing to do with the accident."

"It didn't?"

"Nope. In fact, you may have saved my grandmother's life. Not that it will ever become standard preventive medicine, mind you, but without the accident, Flossie wouldn't have been in the hospital when the symptoms started."

"Oh, Sam!" Tessa drew a horrified breath. "Flossie was that bad?"

Sam gave Tessa a smug look that set her teeth on edge. "Could have been but wasn't. Luckily, she was in a first rate hospital with state of the art diagnostic equipment and neurosurgical facilities."

Deciding that being gracious never killed anyone, Tessa swallowed a pithy response to Sam's blatant campaign rhetoric. "Well, then, I'm glad she was here."

"A polite answer from the saber tongued Ms. Marcovy?" Sam yawned and settled himself more comfortably on the couch. "I must really look like hell."

"Oh, you do," Tessa agreed, her sympathy vanishing. "But I have a firm policy against starting a battle of wits with an unarmed man."

Sam nodded appreciatively. "Ah, that's more like it! I knew you couldn't keep up that sweet facade for long." He rubbed his bloodshot eyes.

"It's a strain." Tessa pulled Sam's unresisting hands away. "Come on," she said gently. "I'll take you home."

"Uh-uh. I'm not going home. Got to keep an eye on Gran. Besides, then you'd have to drive alone from my place to yours." Sam's eyes were closed again. Deep furrows etched his forehead, matching the ones that bracketed his mouth, as if he couldn't stop worrying even while dozing. "Not safe this time of night," he muttered thickly. "So I'll drive you home and then I'll come back to check on Gran, and then I'll . . ."

"Wrong. As tired as you are, I wouldn't let you walk me home, much less drive. As for Flossie . . ." Tessa chuckled as she imagined the nursing staff's response to the news that Eagle Eye Caldwell's grandmother was on their unit. "Trust me, Sam. She's going to get more attention than you can possibly imagine."

"I don't know," he growled. "I can imagine quite a bit."

"Maybe so, but how about if you stop playing God for

a few hours and relax so you don't kill anyone in surgery tomorrow.''

Poor Sam. He looked exhausted. Tessa's hands longed to glide over Sam's forehead and temples in her grand-mother's soothing massage techniques. Her fingers flexed, eager to search out and smooth away the knots of tension in his rigid neck and shoulders. She wanted to erase the stress lines bracketing his mouth and restore the smile whose mere memory made her heart leap again the way it had earlier this evening.

Sam opened his eyes, propped one elbow on the back of the couch, and turned to face Tessa. "I'll check on Gran and then I'll crash in the residents' on-call room . . ."

"Very sensible," Tessa nodded approvingly.

". . . but only if you stay, too."

A night with Sam. All alone. Just the two of them. Tessa wasn't surprised when her stomach did a back flip at the mere idea. *Yes* trembled on her lips until she remembered the last half of Sam's sentence. The residents' on-call room. All the charm of a bus terminal combined with the intimacy of a football locker room at half time. A place where she'd be perfectly safe with Sam. Which was great. Which was terrible. Which was confusing, like everything about this exasperating man.

Tessa gathered the remaining shreds of common sense and shook her head. "Can't do it, Sam. I have a breakfast meeting with Dr. Fowler and I'd like to be wearing some-thing a bit more professional than a Mickey Mouse sweatshirt when I try to nail down his vote for the music therapy budget."

"Too bad you changed out of your white robe. One look and Fowler would have agreed to anything you proposed."

There it was, the wicked grin she had been hoping to see, its voltage undimmed by fatigue. A lightning bolt of pure pleasure shot through her. "Oh sure," she scoffed, "there's something so seductive about a chenille bath-robe."

"There is when you're inside it."

Another lightning bolt zinged after the first one, making her feel a bit light-headed.

"Give it a rest, Dr. Caldwell." Tessa spoke briskly and held out her hand. Ah, good. It wasn't trembling. "My keys, please. And no more nonsense about driving me home."

"God, you're stubborn." Sam grumbled.

Tessa tapped her lips thoughtfully with one finger. "Now *that's* an interesting comment, coming from the man whose idea of compromise is 'let's be reasonable and do it my way.' "

Sam awarded her a reluctant smile. "But you have to admit it would make more sense for you to stay here tonight and run home in the morning."

Tessa shook her head and snapped her fingers impatiently. "I don't have to admit any such thing. Hand over the keys."

Sam patted his scrub suit. "No pockets. I'll have to get them from my locker."

"I'll go with you," Tessa said. "Just so you don't get sidetracked between here and there."

Sam unfolded himself from the low couch and stretched. "Since you mention it, we'll be going right by recovery on the way to my locker . . ." Sam's voice trailed off and Tessa finished the sentence.

". . . so why not check on Flossie." Tessa tilted a smile at him. "Truthfully, I'll feel better if I can take a quick peek at her before I leave. That is," she added, "if you have enough clout to get me into the recovery room."

Sam grabbed the back of Tessa's neck and shook her gently. "Boy, you know which buttons to push, don't you!"

"I'm learning." Tessa shook herself free of Sam's grasp

and walked rapidly down the hall, pondering the whimsical nature of the human heart. Not the heart, she amended. The jolts of pleasure that Sam's touch sent skittering through her were nothing but an annoying hormonal response to an attractive man.

"Let's take the stairs," she called over her shoulder to Sam. "It's only one floor." She didn't wait for him to agree or disagree, but threw open the fire door and trotted up the stairs, her mind still whirling.

Sam Caldwell and Tessa Marcovy! Tessa almost laughed out loud. The mere idea was ludicrous, absurd, a momentary aberration. They were as opposite as two people could be, with nothing in common but affection for Flossie.

Tessa reached the fire door on the next floor and turned, expecting to see Sam behind her. He wasn't. She bent over the stairwell. "Sam?"

"Out here."

It was Sam's voice, but what was he doing on the other side of the fire door? She pushed it open and found Sam across the corridor in front of the recovery room. "You cheated and took the elevator!"

Sam gave her an irritated look. "How the hell can you still be so . . ." He stopped, searching for the right word. ". . . peppy?"

Tessa shrugged. "Lots of waiting room coffee."

"Ah. The legendary prescription strength caffeine." Sam nodded. "With luck, you'll be able to doze off in a week or so."

"Thanks for the reassuring prognosis."

"What's a doctor for?" Sam's tired eyes twinkled at her. "It'll just take a couple of minutes to check on Gran, so wait right here."

Sam disappeared into the recovery room and Tessa leaned against the corridor wall, trying to decide just when she had taken leave of her senses. Was it when Sam smiled at Flossie in the emergency room? Was it during that crazy motorcycle ride when her legs and arms had clung so tightly to Sam? When she realized that a sense of humor lurked under that autocratic exterior? Or when Sam overruled her objections at the house and insisted on coming in?

No, Tessa reminded herself. That was typical infuriating Sam Caldwell behavior. And yet, it *had* been rather nice to lean on somebody else for a change.

Too nice. A glaring violation of her cardinal rule: don't let yourself depend on a man.

Tessa pulled absently at a bit of lint on her black tights. She wasn't depending on Sam; she was working on him. Circumstances had thrown them together, and she was going to change his mind about music therapy.

Granted, she hadn't made much progress this evening, but there was still time. And now that she had analyzed her response to Sam, she could relax, sure that this temporary infatuation would soon burn itself out.

That thought cheered her so much that she greeted Sam's reappearance with a dazzling smile. "How's Flossie doing?"

Sam rubbed the back of his neck and grimaced. "Her vital signs are good, but she's not responsive yet."

"Flossie hasn't been out of surgery very long," Tessa reminded him. "Aren't you expecting too much too soon?"

"Maybe from an ordinary patient, but we're talking about my grandmother."

Tessa glanced at Sam to see if he was joking. He wasn't. "Wow, what an ego!" Tessa hands flew up to her head. "Big, huge, enormous, even for a surgeon!" With every word her hands moved out a little further. "Just because you were there during the procedure, you think Flossie should be sitting up and chatting with you?"

Sam's glacial eyes pierced through her. Tessa suddenly realized how he had gotten his nickname. "I expect her to respond more quickly because she's always had incredible stamina and because her basic health has always been uniformly excellent, like mine."

Sam stood looking at the recovery unit door, so rigid and remote that he could have been mistaken for a statue.

Tessa took pity on him. "I'm sorry. You're really worried." She laid one hand on his arm and Sam shook it off.

"I'm not worried," he said roughly. "A little disappointed, maybe . . ." He looked away and slumped against the wall. "I'm scared to death," he admitted, his voice just barely audible. "Gran's about the only family I've got."

"I understand," Tessa said, feeling a sudden kinship with Sam. It had only been a few years since her grandmother had died and left Tessa alone.

"I'll get your keys," Sam said. "Do you still want to see Gran even though she can't talk?"

"Sure," Tessa said. "She may be able to hear me."

Sam shrugged. "Maybe, maybe not. Anyway, I'll go change while you're in there. I told the staff you might be coming in, so you won't have any trouble." He gave her a quick glance, and Tessa knew that he wanted her to ignore his unexpected outburst. "Gran's in the bed nearest to the nurses' station."

"My goodness, isn't *that* a surprise!" Tessa grinned at Sam. "Run along. I'll stay with Flossie for five or ten minutes and meet you back here."

Sam watched Tessa walk into the recovery room, as bouncy and energetic as if it were three P.M. rather than three A.M. Normally, Sam prided himself on his energy, but tonight he'd be the first to admit that he was tired. Exhausted, in fact.

Checking his watch, Sam reached two conclusions: he'd been awake more hours than he cared to calculate and if he hurried, he'd be able to squeeze in a much needed shower.

Once in the locker room, Sam flipped on the water, stripped off the scrub suit and grabbed a towel. He ran a hand over his chin, hesitated and decided the hell with it. He'd shave in the morning. Right now all he wanted to do was make sure Tessa didn't go all shocky again after seeing Gran in recovery.

If she looked all right, he would escort the pigheaded Ms. Marcovy to her car, make sure she got out of the parking garage without mishap and then gratefully head to the on-call room for a few hours sleep.

Sam stepped into the shower, braced his hands against the wall and let the hot water cascade over his weary body while fragmented memories of the past hours streamed through his mind.

Sam wasn't used to days like this. Not that he didn't love a challenge. Hard work, tough decisions, physical risks— he relished them all and dealt with them in the cool, logical manner that had become second nature to him.

But confronting a medical situation complicated by personal feelings was unfamiliar ground. Sam distrusted emotions. Their inconsistency and unpredictability irritated him. You couldn't see, measure, graph, or chart them. Worst of all, you couldn't draw conclusions and apply them to similar circumstances.

Today he'd been forced through a gauntlet of emotions: fear, anger, compassion, desire, frustration, curiosity, annoyance, amusement, and exhaustion. Running a marathon wearing combat boots would have been easier.

It had been a learning experience. Funny, Sam reflected, how they were invariably painful, tedious, or both. Why didn't learning experiences ever involve trips to Hawaii or free tickets to the Super Bowl?

But he *had* learned something. He was, to use that repulsive psycho-babble term, in touch with his feelings. And right now he was feeling extreme irritation toward Tessa Marcovy.

Sam groped for the soap dispenser on the shower wall and lathered his arms and chest. Why couldn't Tessa understand that he was concerned about her safety and either let him drive her home or agree to stay the night at the hospital?

Her excuses sounded pretty lame to Sam. Sure, he was tired, but it was ridiculous to suggest that he couldn't drive the short round trip from the hospital to her house and back.

And that business about a breakfast meeting with Dr. Fowler was nonsense. Tessa could run home and change in the morning, although Sam knew it was pointless. Fowler hadn't had a new idea since dinosaurs roamed the earth, so Sam could just imagine how receptive he'd be to funding some off the wall department like music therapy.

Sam leaned back against the shower stall and soaped his tired legs and feet, still trying to figure out why Tessa was so insistent on going home.

Sam's sudden grin faded. Tessa couldn't have thought he was coming on to her, could she? He had deliberately suggested the on call room because of its complete lack of privacy. And even if he *was* attracted to her, he was too tired to respond to any woman, much less one wearing a Mickey Mouse sweatshirt.

Still, Sam couldn't help envisioning what was under that sweatshirt. Back at the house, Tessa had changed out of her bathrobe so quickly that she was in the station wagon before he started it. Granted, she was barefoot, carrying her shoes and socks in one hand and running the fingers of the other through her hair. If she had hurried that much, was it likely that she had stopped to put on a bra? Sam didn't think so.

Suddenly Sam realized that Tessa's stubborn refusal to stay at the hospital had given him the narrowest of escapes. Sam knew that if he spent the night on a cot in the same room with Tessa Marcovy, nothing could stop him from holding her, nothing could keep him from kissing her, nothing could deter him from sliding his hands under that sweatshirt and caressing her soft flesh. Not fatigue, not Mickey Mouse's sunny grin, not even, God help him, a trysting place with all the romantic ambiance of Times Square on New Year's Eve.

Nothing could stop him except one word from Tessa: no. Sam was pretty sure she wouldn't say it, not after the kisses they had shared. She hadn't wanted to stop any more than he had.

The unexpected thought was startling, and Sam was suddenly confronted with his body's insistence that it wasn't nearly as tired as his mind was. There was only one way to deal with this latest development. Sam took a deep breath, squared his shoulders and turned up the cold water.

Tessa was secretly disappointed that a shower had evidently washed away Sam's determination to have her stay at the hospital. Instead, he was once again insisting on driving her home and she was once again refusing.

"I thought Flossie looked pretty well, considering she's just had brain surgery," Tessa offered brightly. "Do you mind if I work with her once she's out of recovery? Incorporate music therapy into her post-surgical care?"

Sam shrugged. "It's not my call. Talk to Dr. Weinstein— he's her surgeon, so it's up to him. And I don't distract easily, so quit trying." *Yeah, right, absolutely focused, except for silky pink hair thingies or perfume that smells like a zillion roses.*

Sam and Tessa turned down another deserted hallway, their rubber soled shoes squeaking on the marble floor.

"It's probably just as well you're walking me to the car," Tessa admitted. "When I drive, I usually park in an outside lot several blocks away and take the shuttle to the hospital. I'm not sure I could navigate all the halls and skyways to this parking garage unless I left a trail of bread crumbs."

"The mice would have eaten them by now." Sam looked at Tessa curiously. "Wouldn't it be easier and safer to park in one of the attached garages?"

"And more expensive. Besides, this whole area is pretty safe during the day."

"Aha!" Sam exclaimed. "So you finally admit that it's dangerous for a woman to drive home alone at night!"

"Of course it is! That's why I have a cellular phone."

"Nice try, Ms. Marcovy, but I've been in your car and I didn't see a phone in it."

Tessa threw Sam an exasperated glance. "Mine's portable and unless I need to use it, I keep it in my purse."

"Oh, that's brilliant," Sam said. "And what happens if somebody tries a carjacking while you're stopped at a light? 'Excuse me, sir, but could you wait a minute while I rummage through my purse for my phone?'"

Sam's scratchy falsetto version of a feminine voice was so ludicrous that Tessa couldn't be annoyed at his sarcasm. She dug her elbow into his side. "Okay, you have a point. I should probably have the phone handy whenever I'm driving."

"Change 'probably' to 'definitely' and I'll agree with you. As long as you remember to keep it turned on."

"Didn't Flossie ever teach you about accepting victory graciously?" Tessa grumbled.

"Must have slipped her mind."

They were both laughing as they rounded the final turn into the garage and made their way to Tessa's old wagon.

Tessa unlocked the car, but before she could open it, Sam reached over her shoulder and braced one hand against the door.

"I still think you should let me drive you home," Sam said.

Tessa looked up at him and shook her head slowly. "Sam, I don't want to hurt your feelings, but I think driving with you right now would be a lot scarier than anything I might encounter on the street. Look at you—practically asleep on your feet! I'm practicing basic self-preservation by driving myself."

"Yeah, well, you can't stop me from following you to make sure you get home in one piece."

He was glowering at her, Tessa thought, caught between exasperation and amusement. She supposed she should be grateful that chivalry wasn't dead, but at the moment it was proving to be an annoyance.

"True, but you'll have to walk. You left your motorcycle at my house, remember? And by the time you get there, I'll be in bed trying to come off this caffeine high."

Sam's face fell with ludicrous swiftness and he muttered an earthy monosyllable that made Tessa bite her lips to keep from laughing out loud.

"Look," she said, laying a hand on his shoulder. "You've had a terrible day and a lot of it was because of me, so just this once I'll give into your neurotic need to control. As soon as I get home I'll call the hospital and have you paged. When you answer the page you'll know that I'm okay and then you can roll over and get back to sleep. And tomorrow morning I'll pick you up and drive you to my house to get your motorcycle. So for the second time in the past few hours, good night, Dr. Caldwell."

Tessa reached up to give him a friendly hug and knew instantly that she had made a strategic error. Sam's arms encircled her and pulled her close.

His head dipped lower, a fraction of an inch at a time, as if giving her a chance to be sensible. Tessa swallowed hard, searching for the words and the will power to end this situation. She couldn't find them.

All she could see were Sam's blue eyes searching hers as if they held the answer to an unspoken question. All she could feel was Sam's hard muscled body against hers, so unfamiliar yet so perfectly right. All she could hear was their breathing, quick and ragged.

At last Sam's lips met hers, and all sensations dissolved and flowed into a glowing pool of fire that spread its radiance to every part of her body.

Chapter Six

Tessa shifted in her seat and wished St. Swithin's board could have met in one of the small conference rooms instead of a lecture hall that seated more than two hundred. She slid her damp palms down the skirt of her black linen power suit and then wondered why she had bothered. It wasn't as if she would be shaking hands with every member of the hospital board. All she had to do was get up, make a rational plea for the music therapy budget, and sit down.

The podium placed between the board members and the small audience bore no resemblance to a stage. Piece of cake. No reason at all to be nervous. After all, it was a business meeting, not a performance.

So why were her hands trembling as she again wiped them against her skirt?

"Take a chill pill, Sunshine." Flossie patted Tessa's right hand. "We'll be out of here before you know it with a big

increase for the department. You're not the only one who
knows how to lobby."

Hannah leaned over from the chair in the row behind
Tessa, and put a hand on her shoulder. "And after you
speak, Flossie will add her two cents worth about how you
brought her out of that coma. . . ."

Tessa could feel the color draining from her face. "Oh,
Flossie, you can't. . . ."

Ellen turned around from the seat in front of her and
gave her a mischievous twinkle. "Want to bet? Who's going
to tell the granddaughter of St. Swithin's founder that she
can't say any darn thing. . . ."

"And besides, it's true," Marge added, taking Tessa's
left hand in hers.

Tessa looked around at the four earnest faces. *Surrounded
by white-haired commandos,* she thought affectionately.

"Ladies," she said. "You mustn't forget that I was visiting
Flossie as a friend that day, not as a music therapist."

"Forget?" Hannah exclaimed. "We were there."

"Oh, I wouldn't have missed that moment. . . ."

"When you started singing. . . ."

"loveliest Scottish lullaby. . . ."

"remember my father singing that very. . . ."

"and all of a sudden, Flossie's eyes. . . .

"and she said 'sing the next verse'. . . ."

"a miracle, Sunshine. . . ."

"No." Tessa shook her head. "Coincidence."

"Oh, rubbish." Flossie snorted. "More than three days
after my surgery and all those hot-shot doctors still couldn't
wake me up. Then you came in, sang my favorite song,
and there I was, wide awake and good as new."

"But I did the same thing every day and you didn't wake
up. And the doctor told you that it often takes longer for
older people to recover from the effects of anesthesia."

"It was the song." Ellen reached over the back of her

chair and tapped Tessa's knee for emphasis. "You were clever enough to come up with the right song."

Four pairs of eyes beamed at her. Four mouths turned up in encouraging smiles. Four age-spotted hands patted, stroked, and squeezed her hands, knee, and shoulder.

Tessa opened her mouth to explain further and shut it with a snap. The board members had filed into the conference room and were seating themselves behind the imposing mahogany table at the front of the conference room.

Tessa pulled her hands free and slid them down her skirt again, her nerves stretched taut as harp strings.

Sam came in last, his blue gaze searching the lecture hall until he spotted Tessa. He gave her the briefest of smile and sat down.

Tessa released the breath she hadn't known she was holding and sank back into her chair, certain that Sam was trying to reassure her about the upcoming vote.

She'd done everything she could to make sure her department's budget wasn't cut. Tessa wondered if the board members who had been undecided or frankly opposed ever looked back and realized how often their paths had crossed hers—in the cafeteria, in the halls, and on elevators. She had been charmingly relentless.

Especially with Sam.

Tessa pushed the thought away. Sam's vote was vital, she told herself defensively. That was the only reason she had given him a bit more attention than the others.

No more vital than any other member's vote, came the quick reply. *But did you invite Mrs. Wentworth over for a home cooked meal? Or take old Dr. Frackleton line dancing?*

A sudden image of the octogenarian cardiologist decked out in cowboy gear two-stepped through Tessa's mind, leaving her to convert an inappropriate chuckle into a cough.

Although she might have been better off with Dr.
Frackleton. Even with his walker, he couldn't have danced
worse than Sam.

Or looked as good in blue denim and flannel.

Tessa's mouth went dry at the memory. There should
be some kind of law to keep men with long, lean legs,
powerful thighs, and pattable behinds from wearing tight,
weathered jeans. She wasn't even going to think about the
flannel shirt and Sam's shoulders. She might start hyper-
ventilating if she did.

Tessa risked a glance toward the front of the room and
caught Sam looking at her again.

The butterflies that had been performing aerial maneu-
vers in Tessa's stomach for the past hour continued their
gyrations, but the sensation suddenly changed from nerve-
wracking to delightful.

Tessa sucked in a quick breath as the truth finally hit
her: she was falling in love with Sam.

Her mind raced back over the weeks since Flossie's surgery. She *had* tried to sway Sam's opinion about music
therapy. True, he had only one vote, but the Caldwell
name still carried a great deal of clout at St. Swithin's and
Tessa was afraid Sam's opinion would influence the other
board members. Naturally, Tessa had taken extra pains
with Sam.

Not that it was a hardship. Somehow the kisses they
had shared the night of the accident had been like keys,
opening a door to something that had been locked away
for years.

Once open, however, Tessa found herself reluctant to
close the door again. Not just because of the budget issue
or because of her undeniable attraction to Sam, but
because he made her feel that she might learn to trust
again.

They had started seeing each other whenever their

demanding schedules meshed, usually once or twice a week.

The times they spent together, Tessa thought with amusement, might best be called learning experiences, each trying to teach the other about a facet of his or her life.

Sam had agreed to visit the Rock and Roll Hall of Fame if Tessa would try rafting the rapids in a nearby river.

Tessa had survived a white-knuckled day of rock climbing and unwound that evening by introducing Sam to jazz and blues at a local club.

And, of course, she couldn't forget the ill-fated line dancing lesson at a country western bar. Sam had countered with an afternoon of rollerblading, assuring her that she'd love it.

And she had, although her skating ability was on a par with Sam's terpsichorean efforts.

Their most frequent activity, though, was nothing more than conversation. Tessa marveled that they never ran out of things to say. Often it was a brief, spirited debate at lunch in the hospital cafeteria. More rarely, they indulged in hours of leisurely talk over stuffed cabbage and cheese strudel at Tessa's or perhaps vegetarian Thai delicacies and fresh fruit at Sam's apartment, an unspoken undercurrent of desire adding something extra to the evening.

That was the best learning experience of all, Tessa mused: discovering that the incendiary effect of Sam's mouth on hers hadn't been caused by too much stress and too little sleep. Each kiss they shared sent the same sudden sensation of liquid gold flowing through her veins—familiar, yet always startling in its intensity.

She reveled in the knowledge that her kisses melted Eagle Eye Caldwell's icy exterior, revealing the warm, caring man who lived inside, a man willing to share not just kisses and caresses, but himself; a man who encouraged Tessa to do the same.

And she did, but cautiously, never mentioning the terrible after effects of the concert that had ended her career as a rock singer.

Inevitably, sharing led to caring, caring led to more kisses, kisses led to caresses. And there, by unspoken agreement, it stopped. Tessa wouldn't let their physical relationship go any further while she was trying to influence his decision on the music therapy budget, and she suspected that Sam felt the same.

But after this meeting was over and her department was safe for another year, she and Sam could. . . .

Tessa's flight into fantasy was cut short by a sharp poke from Flossie.

"Okay, Sunshine."

Flossie pointed to the last item on the agenda, which, Tessa thought bitterly, reflected all too accurately the relative importance of music therapy in the board's viewpoint.

"It's almost show time. Get up there and give them the professional's point of view, and then I'll wrench their heartstrings with my story."

"Please, Flossie, don't. . . ."

The chairman cleared his throat and looked down at the agenda in front of him. "The next item concerns a the music therapy department's budget. We'll hear from Tessa Marcovy, who *is* the department at this point in time. She'll explain why she's opposed to the proposed decrease in funding." He gave her a cordial smile and gestured her to the podium.

Tessa returned his smile. The chairman understood the importance of her work and was one of her sure votes.

She took a deep breath, stood, and walked toward the podium, clutching her note cards as if they were tiny little

life preservers and she was on the *Titanic.* The short distance seemed to stretch for miles. Except for an occasional
cough and the soft rustle of agenda pages being turned,
the room was unnervingly silent.

*What do you want? A standing ovation? You're presenting a
budget proposal, not opening for the* Stones. The voice filled
her mind with mocking laughter, the same voice that had
taunted and tormented her every time she tried to perform
after that last disastrous concert.

Good thing, too, the voice continued. *This crowd should
be pretty safe—nobody's high or drunk, so they probably won't
manhandle you if you choke up like you usually do in front of
crowds.*

Tessa reached the podium and stacked the note cards
in front of her. She glanced at the audience and her breath
caught.

Oh, come on, the voice jeered. *There's more empty seats than
people. Even you should be able to cope with that.*

The obnoxious voice was right. So why were her knees
wobbling and tiny beads of sweat trickling down her back?

Of course, the voice said thoughtfully, *the stakes are higher
tonight than they've ever been. Before you just let down the band.
Okay, they were your best friends and it messed up their lives for
a while, but they worked things out. But if you botch things
tonight, you're letting down every one of your patients, present
and future. So do the best you can—you're the only one who can
save this program. Which is a pretty scary thought.*

Once again, Tessa heard a derisive laugh. She wet her
lips and wondered frantically how long she had been standing there. Five seconds? A minute? Three minutes?

"Good evening," she began. "I'm going to tell you about
music therapy's role in the healing process and why if its
budget can't be increased this year, it should at least not
be cut."

Her voice sounded steady enough, Tessa observed gratefully—and promptly lost her train of thought.

Things went downhill rapidly from there. Even to her own ears her hesitant speech sounded wooden, lifeless. Why couldn't she convey the importance of her work with the same passion and sense of urgency she did when talking to individual board members?

With mounting despair, she saw people in the audience shift in their chairs, obviously indifferent to her tedious presentation. She flicked a quick glance at the board members. Their expressions ranged from polite disinterest to smothered yawns. A frown creased Sam's forehead, and his gaze was fixed on the table.

Her speech staggered towards its ending and was met with a smattering of applause, inspired, Tessa was sure, by relief.

She returned to her seat. Flossie's consoling hug told her just how bad the speech had been.

"Okay, Sunshine. You gave them the facts and figures. Now I'll give them the human interest side of the story. And don't worry—they're used to me. I never miss a board meeting and I'm not shy about speaking my mind."

Far from reassuring her, Flossie's words made the hair on the back of Tessa's neck rise up in alarm.

"Flossie, no. . . ." Her plea fell on deaf ears. The elderly woman was already waving her hand briskly at the board members.

A pained expression flitted across the chairman's face, confirming Tessa's worst suspicions. Flossie was obviously regarded as a harmless eccentric, a gadfly whose family connections guaranteed that she would be allowed to speak.

Which she did. At length. Although, Tessa admitted grudgingly, if her own speech had been half as moving as Flossie's, she'd be more optimistic about the board's decision.

She could only hope that the individual board members who had promised to vote for the program would do so. It would be close, though.

The audience rewarded Flossie's remarks with a brisk round of applause, much more enthusiastic than the reception her own speech had received, Tessa reflected ruefully.

Flossie marched back to her seat, beaming with satisfaction.

"You were great," Tessa whispered, squeezing Flossie's hand.

"I was, wasn't I!" Flossie beamed with satisfaction. "Let's just hope that those bozos listened and learned."

Tessa grinned in spite of her worry and wished she could be like Flossie, so sublimely sure of herself.

"Do any others wish to speak on this proposal?" Nobody responded. "Then we'll vote on it," the chairman continued.

Flossie flipped her agenda over and drew a line down the center of the page. On one side she sketched a smiley face; on the other, a sad one. "I'll keep score," she whispered.

The doctor at the far end of the table began. "I vote yes on the budget increase for music therapy."

"That's one!" Flossie made a mark under the smiley face.

"I vote no on the proposal."

Flossie's disgusted snort caused a ripple of amusement in the audience. She put a black mark in the other column.

The vote continued, Tessa's hopes rising and falling with each one. Flossie continued her far from subtle reactions to the voting.

At last it was Sam's turn. The chairman leaned forward and grinned at him.

"Well, Dr. Caldwell, looks like you're the tie-breaker. How do you vote?"

Tessa unclenched her hands, knowing that the music therapy department was safe.

Sam looked at Tessa. "I vote no."

Chapter Seven

Sam stood at the long table, briskly shoving papers into his briefcase, apparently indifferent to the fact that he had cut the heart out of her department.

Rage coiled through Tessa, leaving every muscle taut as a steel spring. Desolation followed in its wake, so overwhelming that her body went limp. The trust she had begun to feel for Sam in the past weeks died instantly, like a fragile flower blasted by a killing frost.

"Don't worry, Sunshine." Flossie took Tessa's cold hand in hers. "We've lost the battle, not the war."

Hannah, Marge, and Ellen all reached for her, murmuring commiseratively.

"Men!"

"Don't have the sense God gave . . ."

"Can't imagine what got . . ."

"Wait until Flossie has a chat . . ."

Tessa closed her eyes and bit her lips. The urge to start screaming was almost overpowering.

"He's coming over . . ."

"Bold as brass . . ."

"Shame!"

The outraged chorus made her eyelids fly open.

Sam stood in the aisle.

"Anybody interested in lunch at Pietro's?" He smiled, curse him, as if it was an ordinary day—an ordinary lunch invitation. "My treat, of course."

"Consolation prize?" Tessa didn't attempt to hide her bitterness. "Don't expect me to be a good loser, Sam."

His smile faded. "What are you talking about?"

Tessa's geriatric support team sprang into vocal action.

"What do you think . . ."

". . . very disappointed, Samuel . . ."

". . . Sunshine told you how important . . ."

". . . have you forgotten . . ."

". . . should be ashamed . . ."

"Ashamed?" Sam's shaggy eyebrows drew down in an ominous frown. "Somebody better start explaining."

Tessa held up her hand to forestall multiple replies. "I guess they're wondering how you could do this."

"Oh, come on, Tessa! You knew how I was going to vote."

"I thought I did, but I was wrong. How *could* you, Sam?"

"Yes, how could you?"

For the first time since Tessa had known them, all four ladies came up with the same line at the same time. Sam didn't seem impressed. He crooked his finger and beckoned to Tessa.

"We need to talk." His icy gaze swept over his grandmother, Hannah, Ellen, and Marge. "Alone."

"Not unless Sunshine wants to." Flossie's eyes, the exact shade of Sam's, were equally cool.

"It's okay," Tessa said. "I'll be right back." She slid past Flossie into the aisle.

Sam led her through a door to an empty corridor outside
the lecture hall, dropped his briefcase on the floor, and
turned to face Tessa.

"Well?"

"Well, what?" Tessa snapped.

"I'm not sure what made you think I would vote for the
music therapy budget, but you obviously need to get the
disappointment out of your system before we go to lunch."
Sam folded his arms across his chest and leaned against
the wall.

"Disappointment!" Tessa could feel an angry flush turning her cheeks hot. "How dare you trivialize what you did
by using such an inappropriate word? Disappointment,
Sam, is what a kid feels when it rains on the Fourth of
July and spoils the fireworks. That word doesn't begin to
describe how it feels to be deceived by somebody you
trusted." She trembled with anger, barely able to keep her
voice low and even.

Sam shook his head impatiently. "You're blowing this
way out of proportion."

"I don't think so. After all the things I showed you—
how the program works, statistics about its effective-
ness. . . ." Her voice broke and she turned away to hide
the tears that sprang to her eyes. "You met some of the
patients, Sam. The faces behind the numbers. Have you
forgotten them? You've taken away something that helped
them to heal."

Sam's hands rested on her shoulders. *Magic hands.* The
thought came quickly, instinctively. She pushed it out of
her mind. There was no magic left between her and Sam
Caldwell. There couldn't be—shouldn't be. Not after what
he had done. But there was.

Sam's strong fingers tightened, turning her around to
face him. "I haven't forgotten a thing, Tessa. But you
have."

"Really?" Tessa slid away from him and stepped back, shocked that his touch still sent shivers through her, despite her anger. "Suppose you tell me just what it is."

Sam's lips tightened. "Before you can heal people, you have to know what's wrong with them. Then you have to keep them alive. If you don't get those two things done, all the music therapy in the world won't help." He jabbed his forefinger at Tessa. "And that's why I voted the way I did—there are better ways to spend the money."

"How can you be so dense?" Tessa grabbed Sam's immaculately tailored lapels. "Sometimes the physical body is beyond help. All we can do is bring peace and healing to a patient's spirit, but in your eyes, that's not enough."

"Damned right it's not enough!"

"Oh, what's the use? Talking isn't going to change anything. The only thing that matters to you is the bottom line." She flattened her palms against his chest and pushed him away from her. "So long, Sam." She turned toward the door.

"What about us, Tessa?"

Sam's quiet question made Tessa pause, her hand on the knob.

"There is no us." She wouldn't look back. If she did, she'd have to face the pain in his eyes, the same pain she heard in his voice.

"I think there is. Unless I was part of your grand campaign to pass the damned budget. Is that all I meant to you? An important vote?"

Tessa blinked back the traitorous tears that once again filled her eyes and gave Sam a long, cool glance over her shoulder. "Believe what you want, Sam. You're very good at that." She opened the door and walked toward the waiting women.

* * *

Sam watched as his grandmother—*his* grandmother!—
the woman who had raised him, the one person whose
loyalty he had never doubted, gave Tessa a consoling hug
while simultaneously aiming a withering stare in his direction.

He closed the door gently, unwilling to let either know
how hurt he was, not even in the subtlest way. Such as
ripping the door from its hinges and hurling it like a
Frisbee through the nearest window.

Sam picked up his briefcase and headed toward the
elevators. As he strode through the labyrinthine halls of
the hospital, various signs reminded him of the grand tour
he had given Tessa just a few weeks ago. Nuclear medicine.
Ultrasound. MRI Lab. CT Lab.

He had even let her observe a non-invasive procedure
designed to measure the flow of blood through damaged
arteries. Experimental now, but likely to replace the riskier
invasive tests in the near future.

And to think he had worried about giving her too much
information.

"Ha!" His disgusted exclamation made several heads
turn. "Not enough!" Staff members leaped out of his way
as if they were gazelles and he was a particularly ravenous
lion, which only annoyed him more.

Why was Tessa Marcovy the only hospital employee he
didn't intimidate? Not that he wanted her to be afraid of
him, but some respect for his superior medical judgment
would be welcome.

"Pigheaded, that's what she is." Sam got on an elevator
and punched the button for the pediatric surgical floor.
"Thinks with her heart instead of her mind." He looked
up and saw several people hesitating outside the elevator.
"Get on if you're going to," he said irritably.

They all stepped back, murmured lame excuses, and scattered. The elevator door closed and Sam was left to ponder his melancholy thoughts in solitary splendor during the brief ride to the pediatric surgical unit.

His mood improved as he visited his young patients and found each one progressing satisfactorily.

Sam knew that he shouldn't play favorites, but he always saw Jimmy Wong last. Twenty years ago, the seven year old would have lost his left leg—or his life—to bone cancer. Today, Sam thought with satisfaction, the technology that failed to impress Tessa had given the boy a chance to live out a normal life span and keep both legs.

He walked into Jimmy's room. The boy's eyes lit up, but he shook his finger at Sam.

"You didn't follow the rule, Dr. Sam. Go back outside and try again."

"Okay," Sam agreed, "but you'll be sorry." He stood outside Jimmy's door and began singing. "A,B,C,D,E,F,G. . . ."

Jimmy clapped his hands over his ears and giggled. "You can come in now."

"If I'm such a bad singer, why do you keep making me do it?"

"You know why! When I'm here, I have to do everything I'm told, even though sometimes things hurt or make me sick. Tessa told me that I'm the boss of my door and I can make people sing a song before I let them in."

"I guess that's only fair." Sam sat down next to Jimmy's bed and passed a gentle hand over the boy's bald head. His role in the boy's recovery was finished, but he still checked on Jimmy each time he was admitted for chemotherapy, hoping that the profound post-surgical depression wouldn't return.

Jimmy chuckled again. "You sing that same dumb song

every day, Dr. Sam. You should get Tessa to teach you something new.''

''She has,'' Sam replied wryly. ''You have no idea how much.''

Sam reached into his briefcase and pulled out the latest book in Jimmy's favorite series of ghost stories—something about a haunted suit of armor. The boy seized it with delight and started reading aloud.

Sam listened absently and reflected that Tessa had not only taught him new things, she had surprised, annoyed, embarrassed, amused, mothered, and teased him. In short, she had taken his orderly emotional life on a roller coaster ride.

Roller coasters. Sam smiled at the memory of Tessa's first ride on one—the cajoling it had taken to get her on the Blue Streak, the oldest, tamest roller coaster in the amusement park. He could still hear her rising voice measuring the coaster's slow ascent up the wooden track.

''I've changed my mind, Sam! Let's turn around. I can't look! Oh, Sammmmmm. . . . . .!''

They rocketed towards the ground. Tessa's body was pressed tight against his, her long hair streaming in the breeze like a black satin banner, white knuckled hands clutching the safety bar so tightly that Sam wondered if the fire department would have to use the jaws of life to pry her loose.

If the astonished backward glances of the other passengers were any gauge, they had never heard a former rock singer scream at the top of her lungs the whole long way down, never taking a breath or diminishing the volume by so much as a decibel.

At the end, Tessa followed Sam off the ride and collapsed against him.

''I'll never forgive you for this, Sam Caldwell.'' Her dark

eyes laughed up into his. "If this is your idea of a nice, tame ride, I'd like to know what you'd consider scary."

"I'll show you." Sam pointed toward a glittering structure that towered over the rest of the park. Screaming riders, suspended by shoulder harnesses from a narrow steel rail, careened around a hairpin turn and down a precipitous incline.

"The Predator." Sam rubbed his hands together. "Brand new this year, so it will be the first time for both of us. We'll hit Maniac Mountain, the Twister, the Mean Machine, Terror Turns, and Space Race first, though. Work our way up to the big time."

Sam glanced down at Tessa and bit back a grin. Her jaw was hanging slack and her gaze was riveted on the Predator's path.

"Unless," he said, "you're chicken."

"Chicken?" Tessa gave a hollow laugh and squared her shoulders, as if preparing for combat. "Why, Sam, I can't wait!"

They did it all, every coaster, every hot dog stand, every corny midway attraction, and got back to Tessa's house late in the evening, hoarse and sunburned—more than willing to collapse on the old wooden swing and rest their tired legs.

Tessa curled up at one end, a stuffed dog almost as big as Ruzsi cradled in her arms. Sam lounged at the other end and Ruzsi sat between them, apparently unfazed by the back and forth motion of the swing.

"Isn't he adorable, Sam?" Tessa stroked the toy dog's plush surface.

"Unusual," Sam conceded. "I don't think I ever saw a fire engine red poodle before."

"He'll brighten up your apartment, that's for sure."

"My . . . no way!" Sam sputtered.

"He's all yours, Sam. You won him, fair and square,

so you get to take him home." Tessa reached over and scratched under Ruzsi's chin. Their furry chaperone eyed the stuffed poodle on Tessa's lap, lifting her upper lip in what looked suspiciously like a sneer.

"I'm not sure Ruzsi is ready to share me with another dog, even one as well behaved as. . . ." Tessa raised a questioning eyebrow at Sam. "What are you going to call him? And use some imagination for once."

Sam gave the stuffed animal a considering look. "How about 'Dustcatcher'? Is that creative enough?"

Tessa's laugh rang out in the quiet night. "Coming from you, Sam, I'd say it's inspired. And you can always call him 'Dusty' for short."

She rubbed her hands over her bare arms and shivered. "I think I left my jacket in the car. Do you want yours, too?"

Sam shook his head. "I'm not cold." He hooked a finger under Ruzsi's collar, unceremoniously slid her to the ground and then moved to Tessa's end of the swing. He put his arm around her shoulders and she snuggled against him, soft curves shifting with every movement of the swing.

Sam's pulse raced and his muscles tightened and his senses swooped in ways no roller coaster designer ever envisioned.

"Mmm." Tessa purred contentedly, leaning her head on his shoulder. "You're nice and warm."

And getting warmer by the second, Sam observed.

Tessa's eyelids fluttered shut, opened and closed again. "I'd better go in." She yawned and nestled closer. "Before I fall. . . ." Her voice trailed off.

Sam waited until he was certain Tessa was asleep before gathering her in his arms and cradling her against him. Her dark hair cascaded over his arm and down to his thigh, the living silk brushing against his skin in delightful torment.

Through a haze of pleasure, Sam thought how seemingly trivial decisions could have important consequences. If he had chosen jeans instead of shorts this morning, he might never have experienced this new and undeniably arousing sensation.

A gentle breeze ruffled a few strands against Tessa's cheek and Sam smoothed them gently from her face.

Sam smiled ruefully. Tessa would be furious if she knew how sleep revealed the vulnerability her breezy manner and irreverent humor masked so well.

His gaze followed the sweet curve of her cheek to her lips, soft and full. They were parted slightly, as if inviting him to sample their sweetness.

He'd wait, though, until Tessa awoke from her nap. One thing was sure—he wasn't suited for the role of Prince Charming. No Sleeping Beauty for him, thank you. He wanted the wide awake princess who eagerly returned kiss for kiss, a far cry from the reluctant woman he had kissed a few weeks ago in this very spot.

Sam wondered what would happen when he passed his physical and rejoined the pararescue reserve unit. Would Tessa be able to handle the stress involved in dating a man involved in such high risk work or would it be. . . .

"The end!"

Sam jumped as Jimmy Wong finished the ghost story and shut the book with a satisfied smack.

"What a cool story! Were you scared, Dr. Sam?"

"Terrified!" Sam produced a believable shudder. "I probably won't sleep at all tonight and it'll be your fault."

He gave the boy a hug, promised to visit when Jimmy returned in a month for his next chemo treatment, and headed for the elevators.

After an interminable wait, one finally arrived, just as Sam decided to walk down the ten flights. It was packed with visitors and staff members.

"Sorry, Doctor." A nurse smiled apologetically. "No room."

Sam didn't even hear her. His eyes were focused on a figure at the back of the elevator.

"Tessa!" Sam ignored the disgruntled muttering that rose from the other passengers when he pushed his way into the elevator, using his briefcase as a wedge to open a space between two burly members of the custodial staff.

Tessa's head jerked up at the sound of his voice. Her face flushed and then paled. "Hold the door, please." Her voice was clear and brittle as glass.

While Sam tried vainly to extricate himself and his briefcase from the log jam of human flesh, Tessa threaded her way to the front of the elevator, jabbed the *door close* button, and slipped through the doors with mere inches to spare.

"Well!" The nurse who had first spoken to Sam whistled respectfully. "Not a happy camper, is she!"

Sam could sense every eye swiveling in his direction. The back of his neck prickled hotly as if the cumulative effect of so many silent stares could cause a physical reaction.

The overloaded elevator lumbered down to the main lobby, stopping at every floor on the way. The ride seemed to take three or four hours. The sardine can confines of the elevator pinned Sam's arm to his side, so he couldn't verify this impression by checking his watch.

Sam was the first one off. Predictably, a torrent of speculative babble erupted from the other passengers as soon as he cleared the elevator doors. He ignored it and stopped to pick up his mail before proceeding to his office.

When he opened his the door and saw who was waiting inside, he almost slammed it shut again.

"Well, Samuel, you've certainly made a mess of things."

Gran.

Sam did a quick visual search of his office, half expecting

the rest of the geriatric SWAT team to pop out of his file cabinets or emerge from under his desk.

But nobody did and Sam breathed a sigh of relief. He only had to deal with his grandmother. Which was more than enough trouble for any one man.

He dropped his briefcase and tossed the mail on his desk.

"What poor sap did you browbeat into letting you in here?"

Flossie shook her head at Sam. "If you ever get a notion to join the diplomatic corps, take my advice and stick to jumping out of airplanes instead."

Sam sat down behind his desk and gestured his grand-mother to a chair in front of it.

Flossie picked up her walker, carried it across the room, and carefully placed it behind the chair before sitting down.

Sam sighed. "Gran, you're supposed to use the walker for support, not carry it around like a purse."

"I keep forgetting." Flossie gave him a guilty grim.

That's it, Sam thought. *Keep her on the defensive.*

"Weren't you and the ladies going to take Tessa to lunch?"

"Actually, *you* were the one who extended the invitation and then left us in the lurch."

Sam's eyebrows lifted at this bizarre interpretation of the facts.

"Under the circumstances, I didn't think anybody would be interested in lunch if I was going to be there."

Flossie snorted derisively. "In other words, like most men, you bailed out rather than talk about the problem at hand. That's how you got into this situation."

"This 'situation' came about because I made a logical decision and voted accordingly. Tessa blew up when I wouldn't let the relationship between us change my vote."

"Wrong." Flossie leaned forward in her chair. "Tessa's hurt because you let her think you were going to vote for the music therapy budget and then didn't."

Sam leaped to his feet. "If she told you that, then she's lying. I showed her this whole hospital from top to bottom; all the new diagnostic and treatment equipment, the research labs—everything. And don't think she didn't do the same thing with me! I even sat in on some therapy sessions."

"And saw Tessa bring me back to normal after my surgery," his grandmother added.

Sam shrugged. "Even Tessa knows that was probably a coincidence." He got up and paced restlessly around the room. "Her work is useful, but budgets are built on priorities, and at this point in time, music therapy isn't at the top of the list."

"Did you ever tell her?" Flossie asked quietly. "Did you ever say, 'I see how much good you're doing with music therapy, but I still feel that other things have to take priority.'" She shook her finger at him. "Remember how in kindergarten there was one day a week when everybody brought something in to share with the class?"

"Sure. Show and tell day."

"Hmm. Show *and* tell, not just 'Show day'?"

Gran's gimlet gaze pinned Sam just as it had twenty years ago when he was trying to make excuses for himself.

"Okay, I get the point." Sam looked away and raked his hand through his hair, frustrated. "But I thought Tessa would be insulted if I spelled things out for her. She's a very bright woman, you know."

He pointed an accusing finger at Flossie. "And I'm not the only poor communicator. Tessa never said, 'I see how important all these things are, but I still feel that music therapy deserves to be funded.' Shouldn't she have told me, too?"

Flossie laughed ruefully. "Darn it, Buddy, you always find the flaw in my arguments."

"Well, now that I'm back to being Buddy instead of Samuel, how about some lunch? You must be starving."

"Thanks, but I've got my work cut out for me if we're going to save music therapy at St. Swithin's."

"Flossie, it's a done deal. There's nothing you can do."

"Nonsense!" Flossie said briskly. "There's always something that can be done. I've already spoken to the Caldwell Foundation people. They can't help this year—their funds have already been allocated. I also offered to fund the department for a year myself, but Sunshine wouldn't hear of it."

"Are you crazy?" Sam was aghast. "You can't afford that kind of money."

Flossie waved her hand dismissively. "Well, she turned me down, so that's the end of it. But there's plenty of grant money out there. Sunshine sent out a bunch of proposals months ago, so she's following up on them while I try to think of a benefit idea that hasn't been done to death." Flossie stood and reached behind the chair for her walker.

Sam raised a warning eyebrow.

"Okay, okay, I won't carry it!" Flossie made her way to the door, leaning on the walker with exaggerated heaviness.

Sam followed her, laughing. But when Flossie reached for the doorknob, Sam put his hand over hers and looked down at her.

"What should I do about Tessa?"

His grandmother paused, considering. "Mmm, I think you should give her a chance to cool off. She's pretty upset."

Sam nodded. "I know. I tried to talk to her in the elevator just a few minutes ago."

"Oh, dear." Flossie winced. "How did it go?"

Sam rolled his eyes and shook his head.

"Just what was the relationship between you and Sun-shine before the board meeting, if I'm not being too nosy?"

"You are, but that's nothing new." Sam grinned to take the sting from his words.

"Well, then?" Flossie's head was tilted, her bright gaze fixed on him expectantly.

"I don't know!" Sam rumpled his hair in frustration. "It's not casual dating anymore, at least not for me. If it comes to a choice between working out and seeing Tessa, I choose her."

"No!" Flossie clapped her hands to her wrinkled cheeks in mock horror. "First step on the road to ruin!"

"Go ahead and laugh, but lately I can't seem to keep my priorities straight."

"Or maybe," Flossie said, her eyes twinkling, "just maybe you've got them straight for the first time in your life." She reached up and patted Sam's cheek. "Don't worry, Buddy. Give it a little time and all this trouble between you and Sunshine will blow over. You'll see."

"Yeah, like Hurricane Andrew blew over Florida," Sam grumbled.

"Lighten up, Flyboy. Oh, and call me if you come up with an innovative idea for a benefit."

Sam snorted. "Don't hold your breath. My idea of a really fun benefit is sending a check and staying home."

"Sorry, It's already been done. By me." Flossie lowered her eyelids modestly. "The No Benefit Benefit. Made a ton of money, too," she added wistfully.

"Have another one," Sam suggested.

"Uh-uh." Flossie shook her head, setting her white curls bobbing. "I never repeat myself."

With a wink and a smile, Flossie opened the door and set off down the hall at a brisk pace, holding the walker carefully in front of her.

Sam shook his head. No use reminding her to use the walker for support—she'd thank him for his advice and do exactly as she pleased.

Which, came the wry thought, was pretty much how he treated Gran's advice.

Sam sat down at his desk and shuffled through the mail. Maybe this time he'd actually listen to her and wait a few days before contacting Tessa. Give her a chance to cool off.

"Junk, junk, and more junk," Sam muttered, and tossed the thick stack of circulars, post cards, and envelopes into the waste basket. As they settled into the metal container, something caught Sam's eye. He retrieved a thin envelope that was stuck to the back of gaudy flyer announcing that Dr. Samantha Coldwheel was eligible to win ten million dollars.

Sam saw nothing but the Air Force seal on the envelope. He tore it open and rapidly read the single sheet inside.

"Your repeat physical has been scheduled. . . ." Sam's mood brightened instantly. "If you are eligible to return to active duty. . . ."

The grin that had spread across his face faded. He read the last sentence again, hoping he had misunderstood its meaning.

"Just what I need!" Sam threw the letter on his desk. "Another complication."

Chapter Eight

"I need some ideas for a fund-raiser, Ruzsi." Tessa gave the dough a few last strokes with the rolling pin. "What's the use of getting matching grants if you don't have the money for them to match? Flossie's stumped, too. Everything's been done before, and we really don't have enough time to plan an elaborate benefit, but a small event won't net enough money to be worthwhile."

She glanced down at the dog, who appeared to be listening attentively. "Faker! You don't give a hoot about my problems. All you want is the scraps from the *kolachke.*"

Ruzsi licked her lips at the last word and eyed Tessa, who was cutting the buttery dough into tiny diamonds.

Tessa spooned fruit and nut fillings into the bits of dough before folding them just as her grandmother had taught her. She transferred the delicate morsels to baking sheets, popped them in the oven, and set the timer.

"Do you realize it's been twelve days since I've seen or heard from Sam?" Tessa gathered some of the dough scraps into a ball and tossed it in Ruzsi's direction. With an effortless leap, the dog caught it in mid-air.

"Not that I care, mind you, after what he did!" She wiped up spilled flour and sugar from the old wooden table and put the mixing bowls and spoons to soak in a sinkful of water. Ruzsi continued searching the floor around the table hopefully.

Strange, how flat life seemed without Sam. Tessa poured herself a cup of peppermint tea and sat down in the nook that she thought of as memory lane.

Several new memories had joined the old familiar photos.

Tessa glanced at the picture wall and smiled in spite of her glum mood. There she was on the great rafting adventure, as Sam had called it, eyes and mouth open wide as the raft plunged through the swirling rapids of a nearby river.

Ruzsi and Sam were playing Frisbee in the next photograph, man and dog looking equally delighted with the game.

The last one, taken by a roving photographer at the amusement park, had caught Tessa with her mouth full of hot dog while Sam wiped a bit of mustard off her nose.

Tessa's heart turned over at the expression in Sam's eyes. A sudden thought occurred to her and she searched the wall of photographs until she found the one she was looking for. It was tucked away in the bottom row, almost hidden by a potted plant.

Setting her cup on the table next to the rocker, Tessa bent down and looked at the picture. A lifetime ago. That's how long it seemed since she and Don had been engaged.

She was standing next to Don in the picture, a broad

smile lighting her face, but not her eyes. Don's arm circled her waist and pulled her against him, but his attention was fixed on somebody outside of camera range.

Tessa took the snapshot from the wall and straightened, looking from the amusement park picture to the one in her hand. How often had Don looked at her with the tenderness that lit Sam's expressive blue eyes? She searched her memory, staring at Don's image, trying to remember, and finally shook her head.

Never. Tessa had seen possessive pride and desire, but never the uncomplicated affection that was so apparent in the picture of her and Sam.

The timer buzzed, snapping Tessa back to the present. She grabbed two pot holders and slid the cookie trays from the oven.

"I've been an idiot, Ruzsi." Tessa transferred the *kolachke* from the trays to wire cooling racks, wondering how she could have compared Sam and Don, when their goals were so very different. Don had cut corners with only one idea in mind: lining his own pockets. Sam was also intent on cutting costs, but she had let anger blind her to his sincere desire to help others.

Her cheeks grew hot as she remembered her behavior toward Sam since the board meeting. At best, she had ignored him. At worst, she had embarrassed him. She groaned, remembering her contemptuous exit from the elevator when Sam greeted her.

"Next time I see Sam at the hospital, Ruzsi, I'm going to apologize."

Ruzsi's tail beat a brisk tattoo, as if applauding Tessa's good sense.

Send him a letter, she told herself. *You don't need to see him to apologize.*

The truth hit Tessa with sudden clarity: she wanted to

see Sam. She wanted to talk to him, to laugh with him, to work out the differences between them . . . to be friends again.

With sudden decision, Tessa pulled a gaily decorated tin from a cupboard and began filling it with the cooling pastries.

"I wonder if Sam knows the old saying, Ruzsi. The one about Greeks bearing gifts." Tessa winked at the dog. "Well, tonight he'd better beware of Hungarians bearing *kolachkes.*

Sam knocked on the door of his grandmother's apartment. It opened so quickly that Sam knew Gran must have been waiting there since she hung up the phone.

"Come in, Sam!"

". . . can't wait to hear . . ."

"We've all been wondering . . ."

"I was losing anyway, so . . ."

Sam backed up against the door instinctively. Helen, Marge, and Ellen waved him towards the dining room table, which was littered with cards and poker chips.

"Flossie," Sam said firmly. "Not one word of my idea do you hear unless all four of you agree not to interrupt me."

"Why, Sam, as if we'd be that rude!" The mournful look in Flossie's eyes would have done credit to a basset hound. She ushered Sam to a chair at the head of the table, sat down next to him, and folded her hands in her lap. "Go ahead, dear."

Sam gave each of the other women a long look. "Everybody understand the ground rules? Nobody but me talks until I ask for comments. Agreed?"

All three nodded, their eyes bright with anticipation.

"Okay." Sam took a deep breath. "I saw a patient yesterday who had a broken arm. A simple break, but he was almost hysterical. It seems his band entered a national contest and won a chance to open for *Uprising* in Chicago a few weeks from now. That's Tessa's old group, you know."

The rolling eyes and muffled sighs told him that, once again, Flossie and her friends were way ahead of him.

"So I started wondering if the group would have time to do a benefit concert here. I explained Tessa's situation to the kid and asked him if he knew how I could contact the band. He told me that nobody named Tessa had ever sung with *Uprising*. So I showed him her picture."

A burst of smothered chuckles earned the four ladies a severe glance.

"I just happened to have one in my wallet," he said defensively.

Four sympathetic nods were accompanied by four broad grins.

"The kid took one look and told me that was Keara, the former lead singer. Once we realized that Tessa and Keara were the same person, he gave me a phone number." Sam leaned forward and folded his hands on the table. "It took me almost twelve hours of calling and explaining and throwing Tessa's—Keara's—name around, but I finally got through to Gavin O'Braidon."

Hannah moaned and fell back in her chair, an expression that Sam could only describe as envious lust on her face. Flossie tapped a scarlet-coated fingernail on the table and gave Hannah a reproving look.

"The band agreed to do a benefit, but it'll have to be something pretty simple—Gavin claims their show involves twenty trucks full of equipment and the schedule's too tight to get them here for our show. He also said that his road manager will give me a list of what they need to put on a bare bones show, but they can't take responsibility for getting or paying for it."

Sam scratched the back of his neck and hesitated. "Here's the fly in the ointment. Even if I had the time, I don't have a clue how to put a benefit together, so I'm hoping you know somebody who'd be willing to step in and take over. I have to let Gavin's manager know tomorrow if the concert is on or off, so I don't have much time."

Flossie, Hannah, Marge, and Ellen leaned forward, eyes shining, gnarled hands gripping the edge of the table in excitement. They looked, Sam thought, like retired race horses lined up at the post for one more Derby.

Sam took a deep breath and wet his lips, preparing to pull his thumb out of the dike, metaphorically speaking.

"So, what do you think of my idea?"

A torrent of words rushed over him as each woman burst forth with her own comments while somehow listening to all the others.

Flossie got up from the table and, still talking, got four legal pads and four pens from a drawer under the china cabinet. She passed them out and each woman began jotting notes.

"I'll talk to the trustees about letting us use . . ."

". . . the old farm! What a good . . ."

". . . arrange for some radio spots . . ."

". . . need lots of flyers . . ."

Sam rapped his knuckles on the table. "Ladies! Quiet!"

"We've been quiet . . ."

". . . asked for comments . . ."

". . . not fair . . ."

"It sounds," Sam bellowed over the din, "as if the four of you are planning to put the concert together. I just want to make sure you know what you're getting into. After all, you're all up in years, and a rock concert. . . ." He shook his head dubiously. "I don't know. It sounds like too much work to me."

Before Flossie could answer for the group, Hannah spoke up.

"The four of us have been friends since high school, Buddy. We ran the Prom Committee back when proms were called cotillions. When we were young wives, we got involved in fund raising for various charities. Learned from the bottom up how to put a benefit together."

"I just thought. . . ."

Hannah silenced Sam with a look and swept on majestically. "We've been doing this sort of thing twice as long as you've been alive. There's more than two centuries of benefit planning experience sitting around this table and you're darned lucky it's available to you." She paused, a mischievous light in her eyes. "And if we're in charge, we'll get to go back stage, right?"

"That's the beauty of being old." Flossie looked around the table with a sly grin. "Who's going to stop us?"

"Well, ladies, thanks again for volunteering." Sam pushed his chair back and stood. "I'm heading for home."

"Volunteering, my foot!" Marge's eyes twinkled at him from behind her bifocals. "You conned us into this, you rascal!"

"Who, me?" Sam grinned at Marge.

"Wait a minute." Flossie put a restraining hand on his arm. "Have you told Tessa?"

Sam shook his head. "I didn't want to get her hopes up before finding out if the idea was feasible."

"Very sensible." Flossie looked up at him. "But since things are settled, why don't you call her right now and tell her the good news?"

Sam checked his watch. "It's awfully late. Why don't you

call her tomorrow? I would, but my schedule is pretty tight."

All four hooted with derisive laughter at his feeble excuse, and Sam grinned sheepishly.

"Tell you what, Buddy. It's about time you and Tessa settled your differences, and this bit of news should help quite a bit. I'll take care of calling her—you rearrange that action-packed schedule of yours and make sure you're at Pietro's by noon tomorrow. We'll finally have that lunch you owe us."

"All right," Sam agreed with mock reluctance. "But I'm counting on you to protect me. She's got one hell of a temper."

"Don't worry." Ellen winked at Sam. "We haven't lost a lunch guest yet."

"Let yourself out, Buddy. We've got a lot of planning to do before tomorrow." Flossie scribbled a note on her legal pad and waved absently in Sam's general direction.

Sam paused at the door, enjoying the sights and sounds of his grandmother and her pals from a safe distance.

"The concert should be wonderful, but I do wish we could see the real road show with all the bells and whistles, don't you?" Hannah's voice quivered with longing.

Flossie slapped her pen down on the table. "Let's do it! After our concert, of course. *Uprising* is playing in New York, L.A., Dallas, New Orleans, and a bunch of other places. Which one sounds good?"

"All of them!"

"Now, ladies, let's be sensible. We can't go to every one." Flossie looked from Hannah to Marge to Ellen. "Can we?"

The women looked back at Flossie. Suddenly all four threw their hands in the air and shouted in unison. "Road trip!"

Sam opened the door and bolted, the groupie grandmothers' laughter following him down the hall.

Although the freeway would have gotten him back to the city in fifteen minutes, Sam turned his motorcycle towards winding back roads instead. Something was niggling at his mind, and he needed time to think.

It wasn't the concert that was causing this uneasy feeling. Everything had fallen into place almost miraculously. Contacting Gavin O'Braidon had been a long shot worthy of a compulsive gambler, but it had paid off.

It wasn't the complex arrangements involved in putting the concert together that had Sam frowning as he navigated the twists and turns of River Road. Flossie and her pals had snatched the reins of power from his unresisting hands, just as he had hoped.

He was still surprised that Gavin O'Braidon had attached one inflexible condition to *Uprising*'s appearance: Tessa had to sing with them. Sam had agreed without a second thought, certain that Gavin wouldn't have made the request if there were hard feelings between Tessa and the other band members.

Tessa, of course, would do anything to save St. Swithin's music therapy department. In fact, she'd probably be grateful to him for giving her the chance to sing with her old friends again.

That was the problem! Sam's mood lightened as he finally realized what was bothering him. He wanted to tell Tessa about the concert by himself, savoring the moment, not at lunch with Flossie and her Greek chorus.

"Lunch!" Sam snorted. "Encounter group would be closer to the mark." He could imagine his grandmother, Ellen, Marge, and Hannah doing their best to bridge the gap between him and Tessa.

Just thinking about it activated a sixth sense that had

often helped him avoid hazardous situations in the military. Apparently this sense worked equally well in civilian life.

Sam gunned the motorcycle and headed towards the freeway. It was time he and Tessa worked out their own problems like two intelligent adults. He was through waiting for her to cool off enough to acknowledge his existence. No more chance encounters at St. Swithin's that left him feeling like something the pest control people should handle. No using Gran as a buffer.

He was going to confront Tessa at her own house, and he wasn't going to leave until they negotiated a truce. The bike roared down the on-ramp to the freeway and Sam pictured the look on Tessa's face when he told her about the benefit concert. At least he wasn't going into this skirmish unarmed.

Tessa stood on the front porch, her resolution fading. Was going over to Sam's apartment really such a good idea? What if he shut the door in her face? Tessa clutched the tin of pastries and took a calming breath.

The sweet scent of the rambling roses that sheltered each end of the porch soothed her, as it always did. Setting the cookie tin on the floor, Tessa broke off a blossom and threaded its stem through the top buttonhole of her camisole.

"For luck," she told herself, brushing a bit of pollen from the delicate fabric. She picked a handful of tightly closed rosebuds and tucked them into the heavy braid that hung over her shoulder.

Everything about her appearance had been carefully chosen to send an unspoken message. "White eyelet, blue gingham, and roses." She unbuttoned the last few buttons on her skirt so the lace-edged petticoat underneath peeped out. "Can't get much less aggressive than that." Straightening the ruffles that barely covered her shoulders, Tessa turned to lock the front door.

A muffled roar from the end of the street made her whirl around. A motorcycle turned the corner at breakneck speed, zoomed into the drive, and came to a halt behind her station wagon.

Chapter Nine

The rider dismounted, removing his leather gloves and gleaming silver helmet.

"Sam." Tessa groaned. She could almost hear the thud of her grand gesture falling flat.

Sam unzipped his leather jacket and strode up the front walk, looking like a young, blond Marlon Brando. His plain white t-shirt was stretched across his muscular torso, the thin cloth revealing as much as it covered.

Tessa tore her gaze from his broad shoulders and washboard abs and found herself focusing on even more dangerous territory. Frayed and faded blue jeans molded the sinful perfection of his powerful thighs and eminently pattable rear.

Sam stopped at the foot of the porch steps and looked up at Tessa. One glance at those heavenly blue eyes, and every line of her carefully worded apology-that-wasn't-an-apology vanished from her mind, along with all semblance of rational thought.

Tessa's mouth went dry, but she moistened her lips and managed a smile. "Well," she said, "you've saved me a trip. I was planning to drop off a high calorie apology at your apartment." She gestured to the cookie tin on the step. "*Kolachke.* Your favorites."

Sam didn't appear to be listening to her. "I stopped by to tell you some good news."

Tessa plunged on, determined to finish what she had to say before she lost her nerve.

"I haven't been very nice to you since the board meeting, Sam. I judged you by the way somebody from my past behaved, and that was wrong. You were only doing what you thought was best."

"Just let me finish, okay?" Without waiting for Tessa to answer, Sam continued. "I've come up with an idea to raise money so you can take advantage of that matching funds grant. Gran and her chums are hard at work on it already."

Tessa rolled her eyes in exasperation. "The least you could do is pay attention when I'm apologizing. . . ." She stopped mid-sentence, sure she had misunderstood Sam. "You've come up with a way to save my department?"

"Don't sound so flabbergasted." Sam grinned up at her. "It's no more unlikely than you apologizing to me."

A cold, hard lump in the pit of Tessa's stomach melted under the warmth of Sam's smile. She turned and unlocked the front door. "Come in," she said. "We'll talk over coffee."

Sam bent and retrieved the cookie tin. "I'll bring the apology."

A four-footed welcoming committee assaulted Sam as he walked through the door, leaping and licking enthusiastically.

"Ruzsi's missed you," Tessa called from the kitchen.

"More than you have, I'll bet." Sam dodged past the dog, wiping the evidence of her affection from his face.

"That's one bet you'd lose." Tessa busied herself with the coffee.

Sam's hands, warm and strong, closed over Tessa's shoulders. "I'd like to lose it." His thumbs rubbed the base of her neck, easing the tension that had become all too familiar since the board meeting.

"What about you, Sam?" Her voice was a husky murmur. "Did you miss me?"

He turned her around and put his hand under her chin, tilting her face up to his. "What do you think?" Sam's ragged laugh conveyed the same longing Tessa read in his eyes.

"I think," she whispered, "you'd better show me how much."

Slowly, almost reluctantly, Sam's lips moved closer and closer to hers. "Are you sure you want to know?" His mouth was just a breath away from hers.

A shiver of anticipation rippled through Tessa as Sam's arms tightened around her. "Very sure."

Sam's lips covered Tessa's in a searing kiss and the world exploded in a kaleidoscope of sensations, changing and shifting from moment to moment, dizzying and delightful.

Tessa's fingers threaded through Sam's hair and trailed down his neck to his broad shoulders. She slid her palms over his back, reveling in the way his muscles quivered under her touch, hoping that this wasn't just another lonely night, another wishful dream.

Sam's questing lips moved to her neck, and Tessa moaned, unable to keep pace with the swirl of feelings his kiss sent racing through her.

Sam raised his head and looked deep into her eyes. "Tessa." A question, a plea, a demand, a hope—all contained in that one softly uttered word.

"Yes." Her answer was quick and sure. "Oh, yes, Sam."

He lifted Tessa effortlessly and carried her up the stairs to her bedroom. To her surprise, Sam didn't put her down immediately.

"I hope you're not in a hurry." Sam punctuated his words with soft kisses on her forehead, her eyelids, her cheeks. "I want to remember every look, every kiss, every touch, and that could take a long, long time, because there's going to be a lot to remember, I promise you."

Tessa looked up at Sam, her eyes dark with desire. "Then maybe we should get started."

Sam's body warned him that he might have made a promise he couldn't keep. He took a deep breath and counted to ten. In Chinese. Twice.

He settled Tessa on the bed, kicked off his boots, and laid down beside her.

"First things first," he murmured, lifting her long braid. His surgeon's fingers quickly unplaited her hair, scattering the little rosebuds as he worked. Once finished, Sam gathered Tessa in his arms and let her hair drift over his skin like a satin wave.

He kissed her, gently at first, and then with increasing urgency as the kiss took on a life of its own, until it seemed as if he had always been kissing Tessa, would always be kissing Tessa. Sam couldn't imagine a better way to spend eternity.

Except, of course, touching Tessa. Her skin was soft and hot under his touch, her pulse quick against his fingertips as they grazed the side of her neck, the inside of her wrist.

Sam's hand slid over the blouse that, in his opinion, concealed far too much of Tessa. Through the delicate material, he felt heat building, muscles tensing, tender flesh tightening.

His fingers encountered a row of tiny buttons, all that

kept him from seeing, touching, and tasting the treasure that was half hidden, half revealed.

Sam unfastened the top button and slid his finger down to the next. He unbuttoned that one and the next before pausing to kiss the soft curves underneath.

Tessa made a soft sound, half gasp, half moan. "Wait!" She pulled his t-shirt free from his jeans, tugged it over his head and tossed it to the floor. "I want to feel you against me." Her fingers trembled as she tried to unfasten the rest of the buttons on her blouse.

Sam lifted her hands and kissed them before placing them around his neck. He then finished unbuttoning her blouse—and found a row of larger buttons marching down the front of her skirt. He hesitated, his hand on the top button.

Tessa pulled Sam's head down and nibbled his ear lobe. "I know you want to take things slowly and remember all the details," she murmured. "But maybe this could be a quick rehearsal." Her dark eyes glowed with desire, but her mouth was curved in a teasing grin. "Sort of make sure we know what we're doing before we start the slow, memorable performance."

"A brilliant suggestion, Ms. Marcovy." Sam wasted no time in unbuttoning her skirt. He tossed it over his shoulder, too fascinated by the scrap of white satin and lace underneath to care where it landed.

Sam traced a line from Tessa's navel to the top of her bikini panties. "As a functional garment, this leaves a lot to be desired."

"But its function is to entice you, Dr. Caldwell." Tessa widened her eyes innocently.

"In that case," Sam conceded, "it's a resounding success."

Sam stood and unbuckled his belt.

"Let me." Shrugging off her blouse, Tessa scrambled

to her knees, and unbuttoned his jeans with some difficulty, biting the tip of her tongue as she concentrated on her task. "I never knew men's jeans were so much harder to unbutton than women's."

"They aren't always," Sam said wryly.

Tessa's eyes widened as he stepped out of his jeans. "Ah," she said. "I see what you mean." She glanced up at him and grinned. "How do guys know what size to buy? I mean, to allow for . . ." she cleared her throat delicately. ". . . expansion and contraction."

Sam grinned back at her. "I think the manufacturers take that into account." He knelt on the bed beside her and twined his hands through her hair, tipping her face up to his. "Any other questions about men's clothing?"

"One more."

Sam groaned. "What is it?"

Tessa ran a fingertip under the elastic waistband of his briefs. "Aren't you awfully warm in these?"

Sam discarded them with one lithe movement. "What about you?" He glanced down at the minuscule garment that accentuated rather than hid her charms.

"Oh, they're perfectly comfortable, thanks." *And you're not,* said Tessa's saucy grin.

"Well, they're making me hot!" Sam growled. He reached down and tried to slide the lacy confection down her legs, but Tessa was too fast for him.

"Missed me!" She waggled her hips provocatively.

"Tease!" Sam's arm snaked out and caught her around the waist. They fell back on the bed, laughing, arms and legs tangling in a mock wrestling match that ended with Tessa pinned under Sam and her bikini panties on the floor with the other clothing.

"Ready for the next part of the rehearsal?" Sam's hand brushed across Tessa's breast and the tip tightened against his palm in silent response.

"As ready as you are." Her hand slid down and touched him tentatively. "Hmm. Not *quite* as ready as you are," she amended.

"You will be," Sam assured her softly.

Tessa closed her eyes and let Sam's lips and hands take her on a journey to a place she'd never been. Her body seemed as weightless as a kite, soaring high, with only Sam's touch to anchor her and keep her from floating away.

She gasped and opened her eyes when Sam's hands moved lower. searching and stroking, testing and teasing, blazing a trail for his lips to follow.

Tessa threaded her fingers through the golden hair on Sam's chest and knew that she had to return some of the incredible pleasure he was giving her. She slid her palms up to his shoulders, holding on to him while she lifted her head and kissed the throbbing pulse at the side of his neck.

Sam caught his breath in a quick, delighted gasp that made Tessa purr with satisfaction. She leaned against the pillow, her fingernails skimming down Sam's back and over his sides to the front of his body, ending with the gentlest of caresses on the hard, hot flesh she found there.

His body's instant response startled Tessa. She hadn't thought it possible for Sam to become more aroused. Obviously, she was wrong.

He rained a feverish series of kisses down the length of her body and back again, his mouth hot against her skin. Tessa arched with pleasure and need, wanting more and more of the delicious shimmering sensation that Sam's touch sent quivering through her.

Finally, he kissed her mouth again, an endless, aching kiss that had her writhing against him, silently begging for release.

"I'm ready," she gasped against his mouth.

"I know." Sam leaned over the side of the bed, pulled a foil packet from his jeans, and tore it open. After a moment he braced his hands beside her shoulders and gazed deep into her eyes. "We're both ready."

He entered her slowly, carefully, prolonging the exquisite moment until Tessa closed her eyes and arched against him, frantic to feel his hot, hard length filling her.

"Open your eyes, Tessa."

Her eyelids lifted obediently. Sam's blue eyes met hers, and Tessa tried to turn her head away from the intensity burning in their depths.

"No." Sam slid one arm behind her neck and tilted her back to face him. "Stay with me, Tessa." His gaze captured hers, making her a willing prisoner as he began moving in slow, steady strokes.

Tessa's body responded instinctively to the rhythm he had set, but it was his eyes, filled with unnameable emotions, that told her their minds and hearts were connected as surely and deeply as their bodies.

Sam and Tessa choreographed their own version of the body's dance, as old as time, as new as now. Joined in love's duet, they savored each intimate delight and anticipated the next moment's bliss, moving faster and faster, until their crescendo was upon them.

They burst into the enchanted space they had created together, where every color was brighter, every scent was sweeter, every sound was clearer—a space that surrounded them for just a few ecstatic moments. Clinging to each other, speaking only with their eyes, Sam and Tessa gradually drifted back to reality.

Seconds, minutes, hours. Tessa didn't know or care how much time had passed. Her world was timeless, reduced to the dimensions of the bed she and Sam were sharing, bodies slick with sweat, breath still ragged, arms and legs still trembling.

"I had no idea." Tessa murmured, stretching cat-like next to Sam.

He propped himself up on one elbow. "Of how seductive you are?" His appreciative gaze caressed the same path his hands and lips had followed earlier.

"Lecher!" Tessa tweaked Sam's nose. "I didn't know what looking into somebody's eyes could do to me. I had no idea that silliness and laughter could be part of making. . . ."

"Making love." Sam finished the phrase for her. "I think that's the big difference between making love and having sex." Sam drew lazy figure eights around Tessa's breasts with a crushed rosebud. "You have to trust a person before you can allow yourself to be emotionally naked, or take a chance on looking foolish in an intimate situation."

"I trust you, Sam," she said, stroking his cheek tenderly. "I may not always agree with you, but I trust you in a way I never expected to trust any man again." She clasped her knees to her chest and rested her chin on them.

Sam shook his head. "Boy, somebody really did a number on you. Who was he?"

"Don Zeigler. The former manager of *Uprising* and my former fiancé."

"Oh, yeah. The slimy bastard who pocketed a goodly chunk of the group's earnings and landed in jail for it."

Tessa stared at Sam, aghast. "I thought you didn't know anything about the group!"

"I did a little research. And the more I read about good old Don, the less thrilled I was. As I recall, you implied that Don and I were cut from the same sleazy bolt of cloth. That hurt!"

"Don't remind me." Tessa winced. "I was so wrong, Sam. There's a world of difference between embezzlement and reallocating budget money. Don was a thief. You're not. It's that simple. But I was too angry to recognize the truth." She sighed. "I guess I used rather inappropriate means to let you know how I felt."

"An interesting way to describe public humiliation in an elevator," Sam mused. "Still, things have a way of turning out for the best."

"They do?" Tessa wasn't sure she believed that little bit of philosophy.

"Sure. People tend to give me more space on elevators than they used to."

Tessa choked back a laugh.

"And even the thing with Don has its bright side. If I had been dealing with him instead of the new manager, I don't think the band would be doing a benefit here in Cleveland for St. Swithin's music therapy department."

"What!" Tessa sat up and stared at Sam, sure she had misunderstood.

"Don't get too excited," Sam cautioned. "It won't be the show that's on tour. Too much equipment to move here, Gavin said. Although I still think he must be exaggerating. Twenty-plus trucks of equipment—come on, now."

"No, that's about right," Tessa confirmed absently. She frowned down at Sam. "You're telling me that *Uprising* is going to do a benefit here?"

Sam nodded.

"And you arranged it?"

"Yup." He gave her a smug grin.

Tessa raised her eyebrows. "How?"

"Piece of cake. Anybody could have done the same thing, given an incredible coincidence, a day off, and the willingness to run up a monumental long distance bill. Not to mention knowing four old ladies who are, at this very moment, planning the whole thing."

Tessa leaned forward, her eyes shining. "When?"

"Three weeks from tonight. Gran and her friends have their work cut out for them."

Tessa leaned against the headboard, almost afraid to believe what she was hearing. "It's really true? Not some creepy practical joke?"

Sam shivered. "Would I play a practical joke on the elevator lady? I don't think so!"

"Oh, Sam, I have to call Flossie right away. We need to discuss where it's going to be, how much the tickets will cost . . ." She leaned across his chest and reached for the portable phone on the bedside table.

"Whoa." Sam grabbed the phone and held it out of reach. "We're supposed to have lunch with Gran and the crew tomorrow at Pietro's. Can it wait until then?"

"I guess so." She gave him a guilty grin. "I'm just so excited—I'm dying to talk to somebody about the concert."

Sam tossed the phone on the floor and pulled Tessa on top of him. "An enthusiastic thank you might work off some of that excitement," he suggested.

Tessa leaned forward and gave him a lingering kiss. "Thank you, Sam, from the bottom of my heart. But tell me the truth—why did you go to all this trouble? Was it just to please me?"

"What do I get if I lie and say that was the reason?" Sam looked at Tessa hopefully.

"I asked for the truth," she said severely.

"The truth?" Sam frowned, considering. "I had a number of reasons, but mostly I did it for people like Jimmy Wong and my grandmother. I don't pretend to understand why or how music therapy works, but I've seen enough to know that it does. And in my opinion, anything that helps patients is worthwhile. So when Gran told me about the matching funds grant, I tried to come up with a real blockbuster of a fund-raiser."

Tessa laughed and kissed him again. "I'd say you've succeeded."

"There was a certain amount of enlightened self-interest involved," Sam confessed. "Where else am I ever going to see you in that sexy leather outfit you used to wear?"

"Sam, I'll wear it sometime when we're alone if you've got some rock singer fantasy, but why on earth would I wear it to the concert?" She made a face. "You can't imagine how uncomfortable those pants are."

Sam shrugged. "Hey, whatever you and Gavin decide on is fine with me. Although," he added, "I may take you up on that offer to wear the leather costume when we're alone. A command performance."

"Why would Gavin give a damn what I wear to the concert? And I don't do performances, command or otherwise, even for you."

"Except for the benefit, right?"

"Wrong." The hair on the back of Tessa's neck stood at attention and she could feel goose bumps popping out on her arms. "Sam, I'm getting a very bad feeling. What's going on?"

Chapter Ten

"Just what I told you. *Uprising* is doing a benefit concert in three weeks and Gavin insists. . . ."

The look on Sam's face told Tessa what was coming next.

". . . that I sing with the group."

"Whew!" Sam whistled under his breath. "I couldn't remember if I had mentioned that, but obviously I did."

"Oh, but you didn't, Sam." Tessa jumped off the bed and snatched her old chenille bathrobe from a hook on the back of the door. "Was that an oversight or a deliberate attempt to force me into singing with *Uprising?*" She thrust her arms into the sleeves and belted the robe around her with a vicious jerk.

Sam swung his legs over the side of the bed and sat there, staring at Tessa in disbelief. "Oh, yeah, it was a big plot. I spent weeks working out the details."

"I wouldn't be surprised." Tessa was on her hands and knees, searching under the bed for her pig slippers.

"You're paranoid, you know that?" Sam grabbed his t-shirt from the floor and pulled it over his head. "I'm tone deaf, Tessa. I couldn't care less if I ever hear you sing, with or without *Uprising.*"

"Well, thank you so very much!" Tessa's voice quivered with wounded outrage.

"Oh, hell, I didn't mean that." Sam rubbed the heels of his hands against his eyes. "I'm just tired and very confused. What's going on, Tessa? Why are you so upset about singing for one night with your old band? Just a few songs, Gavin says."

"'Gavin says, Gavin says.'" Tessa smacked her first against the bedroom door. "Damn him! He has no right to make conditions that involve me."

"No right?" Sam crossed the room in two strides and grabbed Tessa's shoulders. "Reality check, Tessa. Gavin's group is doing a free concert, all proceeds to go to *your* music therapy department, and you won't agree to sing for—what? Twenty minutes? Thirty, at most?" He turned away from her and started putting on the rest of his clothes in sulfurous silence.

Angry tears filled Tessa's eyes, and for one moment she hated Sam. And Gavin, too—everyone who couldn't understand the suffocating fear, the absolute paralysis that gripped her when she stood in front of an audience.

Sam looked up from buckling his belt. "You won't do that much for your patients, Tessa?"

"Not 'won't,' Sam. Can't. I can't sing with *Uprising.*"

Sam responded with an earthy monosyllable. "So maybe your voice isn't what it was a few years ago. That's not the point. Gavin says that fans eat up this kind of reunion stuff—the chance to see you with the group will sell all kinds of tickets. And that's the whole purpose, isn't it? Swallow your pride, Tessa. Put your mouth where you want the money to be."

Tessa gritted her teeth and opened the bedroom door. "Go home, Sam. You're so off-base that you're not even in the ball park."

"Gladly!" Sam brushed past Tessa and ran down the stairs, his boots clattering on the polished wood.

Tessa closed the bedroom door and leaned against it, waiting for the sound of the front door slamming. It didn't come. She was surprised and almost disappointed. Either Sam was exercising amazing self-control or he wasn't as angry as he had appeared.

A faint noise raised a third possibility. Sam might still be in the house.

She opened the door a crack and was greeted by the aroma of brewing coffee.

Tessa ran into the hall and leaned over the bannister. "Samuel Adams Caldwell, get the hell out of my house!" she shouted.

"Not until I get the explanation I deserve," came the muffled reply.

Tessa ran down the stairs and slapped open the swinging door into the kitchen.

"Forget it, Sam. You'd never understand and I don't want to explain, so that's the end of it."

"Wrong answer." Sam shook his head and held out a mug. "Better have some coffee. Sounds like we might be up late tonight."

Tessa clutched a double handful of her hair and growled with frustration. Sam stood across the room, waiting.

She finally looked up at him and nodded. "Okay, I'll explain and you won't understand. Fine." She walked across the room and slumped into the wicker rocking chair.

Sam set the coffee mug next to her and then silently seated himself on a wooden stool at the kitchen table.

"You asked me once if I got hurt during the riot at the *Uprising* concert a few years ago."

"I remember." Sam nodded. "You had a broken arm and some bruises."

"My real injuries, the crippling ones, never healed." Tessa swallowed hard. "They can't be seen, but they've kept me from performing. Every time I went on stage after that, I imagined the audience turning into a mob. I heard injured people screaming for help. I felt hands on me, pulling me into that mass of flesh." She wrapped her arms around herself, shuddering. "Worst of all was the guilt, wondering what we—I—could have done to keep things from getting out of hand."

"I assume you sought professional help."

Tessa gulped a mouthful of coffee. "You name it, I tried it. Psychotherapy, group therapy, desensitization, hypnosis, biofeedback, meditation, anti-depressants, anti-anxiety drugs, vitamins. . . ." She paused, thinking, and then shook her head. "There's probably more, but that's all I remember."

"And nothing worked?"

Tessa jumped out of the rocker and paced back and forth. "Not often and not predictably." She opened the refrigerator door, peered inside, and closed the door again. "I couldn't stand it after a while, Sam. My throat closed up on me so often that people started thinking I had cancer. I fainted on stage once when somebody in the audience set off a firecracker. Gavin told the press it was heat prostration."

Sam shook his head disapprovingly. "Enabling. Very bad idea."

"Spare me the self-help buzz words, Sam. I chose to leave before I turned the group into a freak show. 'What's Keara gonna do tonight, man? Faint? Choke up? Hurl? Hey, man, maybe she'll die! Totally awesome!'"

Tessa turned her eyes away from the pain that flickered across Sam's features during her scathing imitation. "The group deserved better than that. I made the decision to leave so they wouldn't have to do it for me."

"I see." Sam tapped his fingers on the table, apparently lost in thought. He finally sighed and looked at Tessa. "What about the concert?"

"Oh, I'll sweet talk Gavin into doing the concert without me." She sat on the stool next to Sam, smiling confidently. "He'll come around."

"In other words, you'll manipulate Gavin into letting you run away from your problems. Again."

Tessa laughed incredulously. "What problems? They vanished when I stopped performing."

"Wow!" Sam shook his in amazement. "Just like that?"

"Just like that." Tessa snapped her fingers.

"And you never have trouble with things like presentations?" His blue gaze raked over her. "Speaking before the hospital board, for instance?"

"You're despicable!" Tessa's stool clattered to the floor as she lunged toward Sam.

He caught her hand before she could connect with his cheek.

"And you're a coward."

"Well, gosh, Sam, isn't it lucky us ordinary people have heroes like you to admire?"

His face reddened at her sarcasm. "You don't get it. If you're not scared, you can't be brave. This concert is your big chance to break through your fear, face it down and finally put it behind you."

"Easy for you to say—you won't be the one on that stage!" Tessa's hand jerked in Sam's iron grasp, but he held on.

"Listen, when I fractured those vertebrae last year, nobody gave me a prayer of ever getting back to my unit. It took months of therapy and exercise—pain you can't imagine—but I passed the physical. And on top of that,

I've been offered a commission as a regular Air Force officer. That's how much confidence they have in my recovery."

Tessa blinked, trying to tell herself she had misunderstood Sam's words, knowing that she hadn't. *How could you, Sam? How could you make love to me, knowing that you're going to leave?* She wanted to yell and scream and throw things. Instead, she twisted her hand free and managed an indifferent shrug.

"Big deal, Sam. You did exactly what you wanted to do. Hardly the stuff of heroic legends."

"Right!" Sam's eyes lit up. "You're finally getting the picture. All that sort of thing is great, but none of it will matter when I'm standing in the door of an airplane, waiting to make that first jump. You think I won't be scared after more than a year off?"

"What I think," Tessa snapped, "is that you're an adrenaline junkie." She wanted to hurt him, to make him feel as miserable as she did, so it was disappointing when he howled with laughter.

"Adrenaline junkie." His laughter died down into a deep chuckle. "I think I like that better than the Peter Pan syndrome. Remember? You flew that theory by me the night Flossie got hurt."

Tessa's cheeks turned hot with embarrassment, but she lifted her chin defiantly. "So what? It's as true now as it was then. Maybe more so."

"And why is that?" Sam drained his coffee and smacked the mug on the table.

Tessa spread her hands expressively. "You're—what?— thirty years old. . . ."

"Thirty-two," Sam growled. "So what?"

Tessa nodded knowingly, as one who has just proved a point. "You've finally recovered from an injury that could have killed or crippled you, yet you're going right back to the same high risk job. Not just two weekends a month, which would be bad enough, but full-time."

"Not necessarily. . . ."

Tessa held up her hand. "Please, Sam, don't interrupt. I could understand if that was your only option. But you have a wonderful, challenging position at St. Swithin's. Patients who depend on you. Family and friends who care about you." *And a woman loves you and wishes she didn't,* her heart added.

"If it's my turn now, I've only got one thing to say." He slapped his thighs and stood up. "What are you going to do about the concert?"

Tessa shook her head. "We're talking about you, not me."

"No. *I'm* talking about the benefit. You *think* you're talking about me, but what you're really doing is practicing avoidance again." Sam moved closer, and Tessa backed up against the table. "You know what happens when you start running away from your fears?"

"No." Tessa glared at Sam. "But I'm sure you're going to tell me."

"Damn right, I'll tell you! It gets easier and easier to duck scary or uncomfortable situations, and pretty soon you're in a prison that you designed and built yourself."

Tessa yawned and looked pointedly at the kitchen clock. "Well, I'll worry about that when it happens."

"Guess what? It's happening." Sam pulled his wallet from his back pocket and dug through it until he found what he was looking for.

"Here." He threw a scrap of paper on the table. "Gavin's phone number at the hotel. I've done all I can—the rest is up to you." He bent and kissed her forehead. "Let me know how things go." He ambled toward the swinging door as if he hadn't a care in the world.

"That's it? 'Let me know how things go.' That's all you

have to say?'' Tessa put one hand on the table for support, sure that this was a bad joke, that Sam wouldn't really leave.

Sure enough, he snapped his fingers as if he'd forgotten something and turned back to face her.

"As a matter of fact, I've got some words of wisdom for you. First: stop getting your psychological insights from daytime talk shows. Second: solve your own problems before you start doing missionary work on anybody else."

Sam stopped and scratched Ruzsi's ears. "See ya, pal." He gave Tessa a casual wave and left.

Tessa came off the stage, frowning, and was greeted by a medley of upbeat comments.

"... were wonderful!"

"Now that's what I call a sexy ..."

"... outfit like that come in size 22?"

"... great rehearsal, Sunshine ..."

Flossie, Helen, Marge, and Ellen chattered brightly and fussed over Tessa. They adjusted the neckline of her black bodysuit to show a bit more cleavage, straightened the gold-edged, black chiffon panels that formed her skirt, and tucked her hair behind her ears so her dangling gold and crystal earrings would catch the stage lights.

The stage. The rehearsal. Tessa's stomach turned over just thinking about it. She considered bolting to her dressing room, locking the door, and staying there until she died of old age. "You don't have to sugarcoat things, ladies. The rehearsal was a disaster, from start to finish. Can you think of anything that could have gone wrong and didn't?"

"Well," Ellen offered tentatively. "None of the lights fell on the stage."

"That's right," Marge agreed. "And Gavin didn't get

hurt at all when you tripped over your skirt and knocked him down."

"What could be luckier than that?" Flossie asked cheerily. "Oh, and Sunshine, once the sound crew got your body mike working, you could hear every note, even at the back of the meadow."

"Lawn, Flossie, not meadow. How many times do I have to tell you?" Ellen's gentle voice sounded almost testy. "People buy lawn tickets, not meadow tickets."

"Well, it was the meadow when the farm belonged to Sam's grandfather." She looked around at the Caldwell Music Center's outdoor amphitheater and the graceful rise of grass beyond. "Meadows, pastures, and barns. That's all that was here when I was a young bride."

"And aren't we lucky," Tessa inserted tactfully, "that you got us the use of this fine facility for nothing!"

"It's all in who you know," Marge said sagely.

"And what you know," Ellen added.

Flossie grinned wickedly. "It's *what* you know about *who* you know that makes things happen."

"I just hope we can put on a show worthy of this place." Tessa's stomach clenched again.

"I'm sure it will be, Sunshine. The dress rehearsal really wasn't that good." Hannah beamed up at Tessa, who was almost five inches taller than usual in her thigh-high leather boots. "Which is wonderful, if you believe the old saying that a bad rehearsal means a great performance."

"I hope it's true." Tessa held up crossed fingers. "Because if it is, we're going to make rock and roll history tonight."

"That's the spirit!"

"and we'll be here . . ."

". . . I've got my video camera . . ."

Tessa's smile faded. "I forgot about the video crew." She winced. "And the recording people."

"We didn't." Flossie said smugly. "We'll still be raking it in from the video and the live album long after the concert's over."

Tessa looked at her four friends affectionately, and shook her head. "I'll never, never know how you pulled this all together in three weeks."

"Well, dear, once we got over the silly notion that we needed six hours sleep to function . . ."

"That's eight hours," Tessa said severely. "Not six."

The four ladies looked at each other and shrugged. "Good thing we didn't know that or we'd *really* have been tired!"

They laughed merrily.

"And when you get to be our age, you've got a lot of markers you can call in, so that was a big help."

"That's right, Hannah, and of course we all have *very* good memories and lots of stories we could tell if we were so inclined . . ." Ellen's smile was innocent enough, but her eyes sparkled with mischief.

"Have you ladies been blackmailing people again?"

Sam's voice sent Tessa's stomach lurching up into her throat and then plunging to her knees. It wasn't a comfortable feeling.

Flossie chuckled. "Oh, Sam, you know how Ellen exaggerates. We made a few phone calls and every single person we talked to remembered us and wanted to help." She heaved a sentimental sigh. "Such generosity!"

"Oh, lord." Sam groaned and shaded his eyes with one hand. His intended audience didn't notice. Their attention was riveted on Gavin O'Braidon, standing alone at the center of the stage.

"Flossie, what. . . ."

"Later, Sam." His grandmother waved a dismissive hand as the four ladies trotted closer to the stage.

Tessa and Sam were left alone, wearing the strained

smiles of those who have been lovers, but aren't quite sure what their current status is and don't want to ask for fear of hearing something unpleasant.

Tessa searched for a clever icebreaker. "So!" she said. "Here you are!"

Sam's smile was as artificial as saccharin. "Yup, I am."

Which pretty much exhausted that topic. Tessa cast about for another. "Flossie said you'd come, but I wasn't sure."

"I might not have, if you hadn't sent me a ticket."

Sam must have seen the bewildered look that flashed across her face, because he grinned ruefully and said, "Flossie."

"Who else?" Tessa responded.

They both laughed, easing the tension somewhat.

"How's it feel, being back on stage?"

Tessa wanted to hurl herself into Sam's arms and tell him how awful the rehearsal had been and how terrified she was of the upcoming performance. "Great! Much easier than I expected."

"Good." Sam nodded absently and frowned. "Can you move around in those orthopedic nightmares?" He pointed to her boots.

"As much as I need to." Knees bent, she planted her feet about shoulder width apart and executed a series of lazy figure eights with her hips. The black chiffon panels of her skirt swirled and separated, revealing the sleek boot-clad length of her legs.

"Holy. . . ." Sam's eyes widened.

Tessa brought her feet closer together and shimmied toward Sam, every part of her body moving in one sinuous ripple.

Sam swallowed hard.

"See?" Tessa said brightly. "Piece of cake." *Unless I trip and fall on Gavin again,* Tessa pushed the thought away. She'd get through the performance. She had to.

"How do you like the rest of the costume?" She twirled around to give him the full view. *Eat your heart out, Sam.*

"Well, Ms. Marcovy." Sam surveyed her costume piece by piece. "It's not very functional."

Something in Sam's voice told Tessa that he was remembering the last time he had spoken these words to her. She felt a blush start somewhere around her navel.

"Its function, Dr. Caldwell, is to . . ." She met Sam's eyes and glanced away. ". . . entertain the audience." *Oh, Sam, why couldn't I let you know that I remember, too?*

"I'll let you know how well it measures up." Sam gave her a cocktail party smile, bland and smooth.

"So you're staying for the show, then." *I can be just as superficial as you can, Dr. Caldwell.*

"At least until you sing. I wouldn't miss that."

Tessa laughed. "Poor you! I'm on last."

"Well worth the wait, I'm sure."

"I'll try not to disappoint you." *Ken and Barbie probably have deeper conversations than this,* Tessa thought despairingly. Was it only three weeks ago that she had been naked in Sam's arms, their bodies and souls fused together?

"Sunshine!" Flossie beckoned to Tessa from her vantage point near the stage. "They want you out there with Gavin for a few pictures."

"In a minute," Tessa called over her shoulder.

She turned back to Sam and held out her hand. "Gotta run, but I'll look for you when I come on stage."

"Front row center. Can't miss me." Sam took her hand and his smile faded. "Your hand is like ice!" He looked at her intently. "Pre-show jitters?"

Her smile wavered. "You could say that."

Sam reached for her other hand and held them both in his. "Hey, don't worry."

Tessa could have cried at the tenderness in his voice.

"You know what? Even if you go out there and forget the lyrics, or throw up, or faint and fall flat on your face, it doesn't matter at all."

"It doesn't?" Tessa looked up at Sam. The expression in his eyes warmed her heart. *Because I'll love you no matter what, Tessa.*" She closed her eyes and waited for Sam to say the words aloud.

"Not a bit. You've already got the ticket money, so the department is safe. Who cares what happens now?"

Tessa's eyes popped open and she snatched her hands away from Sam's. "Gosh, Sam, that makes me feel ever so much better." She glared at him, and stalked toward the stage.

Sam followed her. "Tessa," he said softly.

She stopped, but didn't turn around. "What?"

Sam stepped in front of her and pressed his lips to hers. "For luck," he murmured.

Tessa swayed towards Sam, her fingertips brushing against her mouth, her luminous gaze searching his eyes.

A shout from the stage made Tessa jump. "Thanks, Sam." She dodged past him and ran out on the stage towards Gavin.

A crew from a local TV station did a brief interview with Tessa and Gavin. Sam watched, fascinated. Even though he had seen a picture of her in costume, he couldn't quite get used to the transformation of Tessa, the music therapist, into Keara, the rock singer.

In her costume and stage make-up, she was exotic and seductive, shining and glimmering under the lights like a fantasy come to life.

One thing remained the same: he had a knack for annoying Keara just as surely as Tessa. He replayed their conversation in his mind and shook his head, bewildered. The concert was a sell-out and the tickets were non-refundable. Logically, there were no real reasons for stage fright. The money was safe, and a bad performance couldn't wreck a career that had ended three years ago. He had pointed that out to reassure Tessa . . . Keara. Why had she gotten so testy?

At least he had kissed her for luck. She'd never know how hard it had been to keep that kiss brief and uncomplicated when what he really wanted to do was wrap his arms around her and tell her how much he loved her and that he had turned down the opportunity to make the Air Force a full time career. He wanted to suggest eloping immediately after the show, followed by a quick honeymoon on some tropic isle. Nothing excessive—a year or so would do.

Sam took a deep breath. At least he had been smart enough to keep it simple. The last thing Tessa or Keara needed right now was another complication.

Sam filled his eyes with one more look at her loveliness before heading for the front of the amphitheater. Time enough to tell her what was in his heart after the concert was over.

Marriage. Although Sam had never thought about it much, he had always assumed that he would get married sometime in the future. The far distant future, preferably, after he was too old to care about adventure.

Sam chuckled. Living with Tessa, he suspected, would be a never-ending adventure. He couldn't wait.

He wondered how much convincing it would take before she agreed to marry him. It didn't matter, Sam told himself. He loved a challenge.

Two men were talking earnestly to the right of Sam. When he heard them mention Keara, he deliberately slowed his pace, eavesdropping aimlessly.

The middle-aged man in the power suit and Italian shoes looked worried. ''I'm having second thoughts about the recording contract after that dress rehearsal. Not good, not good at all.''

"Get over it, mate." The second man was obviously a band member. If the guitar slung over his shoulder wasn't enough of a tip-off, his thick Irish brogue certainly was. "If our Keara didn't bomb the dress rehearsal, we'd probably cancel the show. She always botches the practice and steals the damn show."

The older man shook his head. "We'll see."

"Yeah, well, you'll likely see Keara on tour with us this fall. Gavin's already asked her and she's just about ready to say yes. Seems this Air Force boy-o has busted her heart. . . ." He glanced at Sam, lowered his voice, and continued his story.

Chapter Eleven

Sam walked on, feeling as though he had just jumped from a plane and discovered that his parachute was still inside. How had he broken her heart? He stopped short, as a horrible thought ripped through his mind. Could it be some other Air Force guy?

He shook his head, remembering the magic he and Tessa had shared for too brief a time. There was no other man in her life, he'd bet his own on that. Sure, their passionate encounter had ended badly, but Sam had deliberately chosen to wait until life returned to normal after the concert before trying to straighten things out.

At the time, it had seemed a sensible plan. In retrospect, it appeared to have been a major tactical blunder.

But still, Tessa going back on the road? A farfetched notion, considering how unequivocally she had refused to appear at the benefit. Yet here she was, in costume and all ready to perform, in spite of her fear. Could it be an over-reaction to their little spat. All right, Sam acknowledged, to their major blow-up.

Didn't Tessa realize that he loved her? That he only pushed her to conquer the fear so she could use all her talents to the fullest?

Sam tripped on something bulky. A quick look around told him that he was near the back of the lawn seating area. He glanced down, wondering what he had stumbled over and saw an outraged couple clutching a picnic basket. As if, Sam thought, he was planning to grab it and dash off into the bushes that surrounded Caldwell Music Center's lawn.

The broad grassy area was filling up with picnickers stretched out on blankets, enjoying an al fresco dinner while waiting for the show to start.

Sam headed back toward the amphitheater, trying to figure out just what he would say to Tessa after the concert. Something that would convince her of his love and change her mind about going on tour.

He tried out a rough draft under his breath. "Tessa, don't go on tour. I love you, I need you, I can't live without you."

"Are you talking to my woman?" A Hulk Hogan look-alike gave Sam a menacing stare.

"Of course not," Sam snapped.

"Oh, I'm not good enough for you, pretty boy?" The woman, who could have been the centerfold in any issue of *Biker Babes,* was even scarier than her boyfriend.

Sam's legendary survival instincts kicked in. "No, dear lady." Sam took her hand and bowed gallantly over it. "I'm not good enough for you."

He hastened on, not waiting to gauge the effect of his reply. Words were slippery things, he reflected, easily misinterpreted. Probably why the old saying, actions speak louder than words, was still around. That's what he needed, an action, a physical gesture that Tessa couldn't misinterpret.

Something like slaying a dragon, or throwing his cloak across a puddle. Unfortunately, the twilight sky was cloudless, offering no chance of a downpour that might create a suitable puddle. There was a conspicuous absence of dragons, too. Plenty of frogs croaking in the ponds that dotted the grounds, but Sam suspected that slaying a frog wasn't going to dazzle the fair maiden in his life.

No, what he needed was a bold plan that combined action *and* words. But what? He continued analyzing and discarding possibilities.

"Aha!" Sam clapped his hands together and chuckled. Several couples in his path quietly moved their blankets and coolers.

"Hey, no problem. I just had this great idea, and. . . ." Sam shrugged. Not much point in explaining if people weren't going to stick around and listen. Too bad. This idea had real promise except for two flaws: it would take time and a talented helper.

Sam glanced at the empty stage and checked his watch. With any luck at all, he could set everything up and still see Tessa perform. He started running for the parking lot. No time to waste!

Tessa emerged from her dressing room on unsteady legs.

"Tummy gone wonky again?" Billy, the British manager of *Uprising*, gave her a sympathetic pat on the back.

Tessa scorched him with a look that would have welded a lesser man's mouth shut. "I was touching up my make-up."

"With all the touching up you've done tonight, love, your face must be a good inch larger all round." Billy sighed wistfully. "I just wish I'd thought to install a coin lock on the loo. I could have retired tonight, a rich man."

Tessa snorted. "A vulgar one, I'd say." She winked at Billy to let him know it was her nerves talking and not her.

Billy returned the wink. "Five minutes, love." He moved away, knowing she needed time alone to collect her thoughts.

Her thoughts stubbornly refused to be collected. Tessa felt like a cowboy with a particularly recalcitrant herd of cattle. As fast as she got one corralled, three more would go leaping off in another direction.

Images of Sam collided with panicky thoughts about the concert. *Oh, Sam—your eyes—I could drown in them. What if my voice cracks? Kiss me again, Sam. I love you! Maybe the audience won't remember me. Don't go away, Sam. I need you more than the Air Force does. My legs are numb. Oh, no! It's hysterical paralysis! I won't be able to walk on stage! I'll be fine— Sam's waiting in the front row.*

Tessa closed her eyes and took several deep breaths, focusing on the image of Sam, front row, center seat, his eyes looking up at her, warm and encouraging, lending her strength.

"You're on, love!" Billy folded her nerveless fingers around a tambourine and gave her a gentle shove in the direction of the colored lights and the swirl of clouds from a fog machine.

And then she was out there, at the back of the stage, moving to the pounding rhythm of the drums as Gavin and the others tore into the opening bars of *Drive Me to the Edge,* one of the band's first big hits.

As she danced toward Gavin, Tessa flicked a quick glance at the front row. There were Marge, Hannah, Ellen, Flossie—and an empty seat. Tessa stumbled slightly and even over the music, she could hear a murmur sweep through the audience.

Her stomach turned over and her head felt like an over-inflated balloon. *Where's Sam? I can't do this without him! He promised he'd be here.*

Gavin's bad boy grin greeted Tessa as she danced up to him, but his eyes were worried. Waves of sound roared up from the audience, crashing against Tessa, over and over.

She glanced down at the audience, hoping to spot Sam in another row—and almost lost her balance again.

"Keara! Keara! Keara!" The audience was standing, chanting her name.

Tessa glanced around at the members of the band. They were grinning at her, playing the intro to the song over and over, clearly enjoying her stupendous reception, waiting for her signal to move into the song.

And suddenly Tessa knew why she had to do this concert. It wasn't for Flossie or the band or Sam or the audience or even the future of St. Swithin's music therapy department. She had to do this concert for herself—to find the person who had disappeared into that out of control mob three years ago and had hidden away ever since.

Tessa twirled around and crashed the tambourine against the palm of her hand. The band answered with a power chord that would have pulled the audience out of their seats if they hadn't already been standing. Tessa saw Gavin's usual audacious twinkle wipe away the worried look in his eyes as they harmonized on the first verse of the song.

The music swept through Tessa's veins, wild and hot, filling her with a barely remembered exultation, a feeling like nothing else she knew.

Tessa flirted shamelessly with the audience, singing, dancing, swooping, swirling, half drunk on the power she had over them, reluctant to let it go.

Towards the end of the concert, the lights dimmed and Gavin put his electric guitar aside in favor of an old acoustic instrument. Tessa stood in the spotlight, holding a hand mike.

"I'd like to sing something I wrote just recently." She smiled down at the hushed audience. "It's called *My Only Home is You* and I'm doing it for somebody special who couldn't make it tonight. I'm hoping he'll hear it on the radio simulcast since I wrote it for him."

She sang it simply, her pure voice ringing like silver and crystal, telling the story of a woman who would leave everything to be with the man she loved. When the song ended, the audience gave her the ultimate compliment— seconds of silence followed by thunderous applause.

Nobody wanted the concert to end. The last song on the play list, the last scheduled encore, the fifth unscheduled encore—all had been played, and still the audience stood, clamoring for more, their voices almost as hoarse as those of the band members.

"One more," Tessa pleaded. "I'm fine."

"Get over it," Gavin rasped. "You've only been singing for an hour—we've been up here for two." He grinned at the audience, touching his throat and shrugging helplessly. "You can sing to your heart's content on the road tour," he reminded her, slinging an affectionate arm over her shoulders.

Tessa allowed Gavin to lead her off-stage, grateful for his arm around her. Without it she might have soared into the night sky on a once in a lifetime high.

Was this how Sam's pararescue work made him feel? In control, powerful, able to take any risk and beat the odds? Was it fair to hope that he would leave that job for the safer world of hospital medicine?

Tessa stopped short. "Go on without me," she told Gavin. "I have to make a call."

"Trackin' down lover boy, are you?" Gavin grinned at

her. "Where'd he disappear to? I thought he was going to be right down in front."

"That's the question I want answered." She kissed Gavin's cheek and ran toward her dressing room. "I'll see you at the party."

Five minutes later, Tessa was still sitting in her dressing room, trying to make sense of what she had learned from her phone call to Gavin's service.

"Tessa?" Flossie called from outside. "Are you in there? And if you are, why?"

Tessa opened the dressing room door and was engulfed in four smothering hugs.

"Fabulous!"

". . . so proud . . ."

". . . best show I've ever . . ."

"Outta sight!"

"Tonight wouldn't have happened without you." Tears filled Tessa's eyes. "And Sam," she added.

"No tears, Sunshine." Flossie whipped a lace edged handkerchief from her purse and blotted them carefully. "Can't let Sam see you with zebra stripes running down your face."

"Is he here?" Tessa asked eagerly. "I didn't see him with you in the front row."

"Not yet. Poor Sam!" Ellen clucked her tongue sympathetically. "He must have gotten an emergency call from the hospital."

"Doctors' wives have to get used to being abandoned." Flossie winked conspiratorially. "I know!"

"He's not at the hospital, Flossie. He's not even on call. He told his service he wouldn't be answering any pages tonight. because he was going to be at the concert."

Flossie frowned. "Then where the heck is he?"

* * *

"I can't believe this is happening again!" Sam slapped the steering wheel, frustrated. "I got caught in the incoming traffic when I left, and now I'm stuck waiting for the damned outgoing traffic to clear up. What the hell could be taking so long? The concert's been over for at least thirty minutes."

Juan Rodriguez laughed. "Never been to a concert here, have you, doc?"

"No." Sam gritted the words between his teeth. "So what?"

"It takes more than an hour for the parking lot to empty."

Sam shook his head. "I can't wait that long. The party might be over before we get in there." He cast a sulfurous look at the policemen directing the double lines of cars streaming from the parking lot and made a quick decision.

"I'm going to talk to one of the cops," he told Juan. "There has to be another entrance into the complex."

Juan laid a restraining hand on Sam's sleeve. "I don't think that's such a good idea, doc, not the way. . . ."

Sam shook Juan's hand off and jumped out of the car.

". . . you're dressed." Juan shrugged philosophically and waited.

Sam sized up the situation and figured he'd have a better chance with the female officer. He strolled over to her and smiled. "Excuse me, ma'am, but I have to get down to the amphitheater."

She glanced up at Sam and her eyes widened. "Gonna have to wait until these cars clear out."

"I need to find the emergency entrance. I'm a doctor."

"Yeah? What's the emergency? A wounded bull?"

Great, Sam thought. *Just what I need—a cop who thinks she's a comedian.*

"I'm a doctor," he repeated carefully. "A people doctor, not a vet."

"Sorry." She waved her flashlight vigorously at the exiting cars. "The bullfighter's suit kind of threw me off."

"This is a costume." Sam looked down at his outfit and back at the cop. "I'm dressed as a troubadour."

"Troubadour, huh? Don't your patients think a doctor in costume is a little . . ." She waved another batch of cars on, evidently searching for just the right word. ". . . a little odd?"

Sam glared at her. "Are you going to tell me where the emergency access is?"

"Nope." She jerked a thumb at his car. "Inside, Dr. Troubadour. This mess should be cleared up in an hour or so. If you get bored," she called after Sam, "try humming a few show tunes." Her hearty laugh accompanied him back to the car.

"So where can we get in?" Juan asked.

"She wouldn't tell me." Sam slid into the driver's seat and crossed his arms on the steering wheel, brooding. "Can you believe that cop thought I was wearing a bull-fighter's outfit?"

Juan nodded. "You are."

"Are you nuts, too? I told the guy at the costume shop that I wanted to look like a troubadour."

"Troubadour, toreador—kind of close, you know?"

"What the hell's a toreador?" Sam demanded.

"Spanish for bullfighter."

"No, Juan, the Spanish word for bullfighter is matador. And I know I'm right," Sam said firmly, "because I've been to Mexico and almost went to a bullfight."

"Me too," said Juan. "Been to Mexico, I mean. In fact, I was born there. See, there's different words for different kinds of bullfighters. A matador usually fights on foot and a toreador is more often on a horse, while a picador. . . ."

Sam raised his hand and halted the stream of information. "Different kinds." He stared out the window, tapping his fingers on the steering wheel. "I must look pretty silly."

"No, no," Juan assured Sam earnestly. "You look quite handsome. Not every man has the legs for a suit of lights."

"I thought when I rented it that it seemed a little gaudy, not casual enough for a troubadour, somehow."

Juan nodded in silent agreement.

Sam saw the female police officer talking into her walkie-talkie and gesturing at his car. The officer on the other side of the road listened and peered through the traffic. They both laughed.

The last shred of Sam's patience unraveled. "I'm not waiting for another hour, minute, or second. We're going to get to that party on foot." His voice brooked no argument.

"It's a pretty long walk," Juan commented.

"That's why we're going to run," Sam said grimly. "Any problems with that?"

"Not at all, doc." Juan reached into the back of Sam's car, pulled out a guitar and slung it over his shoulder.

The police officer spotted them as they headed through the trees in the direction of the pavilion. "Hey, Doc Troubador!" she yelled. "Get back here or I'll have your car towed."

"Be my guest," he shouted over his shoulder. Sam ran on, with Juan puffing a few yards behind him.

For a party planned in less than three weeks, it was spectacular. Plenty to eat, plenty to drink, and an air of euphoria about the whole event.

Although the party was limited to the volunteers who had helped set up the concert and the donors of equipment and services, many people were fans of *Uprising*. Tessa

signed autographs, posed for pictures, and explained that
nothing had been decided about her joining the tour.

Her eyes kept scanning the crowd, hoping that she would
spot Sam drifting in from . . . where?

Tessa slipped away twice to call Sam's service, but they
had nothing more to tell her. She described him to the
security guards and asked them to tell her if he showed
up at the party.

All the praise, all the compliments, all the questions
about her future with the group flowed in one ear and
out the other, without making the slightest impression.
Tessa couldn't think of anything but Sam's mysterious dis-
appearance from the concert.

Gavin strolled up and handed her a glass. "Have a drink
and brighten up, dear heart. It's a party, not a wake. We've
just finished one of the great reunion concerts of all time,
and you're walking round with a face so long you could
eat oats out of a churn."

"Sam still hasn't come back, Gavin. What on earth could
have happened to him?"

"Did he say he'd meet you at the party?"

"He must have." Tessa tried to reconstruct the conversation between her and Sam before the show. She looked
at Gavin, stunned. "He didn't. All he said was that he'd
be sitting front row center and that he'd stay until I sang."

Gavin raised his eyebrows. "Nothing about the party?"

"Not a word."

"Hmmm." Gavin thought for a moment. "There's a
number of reasons he might not have been in the front
row for you."

"Like what?" Tessa crossed her arms and waited.

"He could have been so nervous about your performance that he couldn't sit that far away from the gents'
room."

Tessa laughed. "Come on, Gavin. You can do better than that!

"I wouldn't discount that theory, love." His eyes twinkled at Tessa. "Some of the crew had a pool going to see how many pit stops you made before the performance."

"Oh, yuk! That's degrading!" She glanced at Gavin. "I'll bet Billy won."

"Just like he used to in the old days, and if you're smart, you'll demand a percentage of his winnings for your matching funds grant."

They both burst out laughing.

"A second possibility," Gavin said, "is that he couldn't stand the noise. He's not much of a concert-goer, is he?"

Tessa rolled her eyes. "That's an understatement of monumental proportions."

"Well, there you are!" Gavin spread his hands. "Imagine sitting in the front row for your first concert. It's lucky the poor sod wasn't deafened on the spot. He may have started out in the front row and moved in an attempt to preserve his hearing, not to mention his sanity, with all those screaming fans."

"But why wouldn't he come to the party?" Tessa bit her lip, trying to imagine where Sam could be.

Gavin put his arm around Tessa's waist and pulled her close. "If I were in his shoes, I'd give the party a miss and go to the lady's house. Wait for her there as long as it took. Seems like it would be worth the wait to get her to meself, particularly if I hadn't been alone with the lady for several weeks."

Tessa put her hands on Gavin's shoulders, and kissed him gleefully. "I think you're right on target. I'll bet Sam's sitting on my front porch swing right this minute, wondering what's taking me so long."

"Well, what are you waiting for?" Gavin patted her behind. "Take off, make tracks, hit the road!"

"I will!" She started toward her dressing room.

"Where the devil are you going?" Gavin called after her.

"To take a shower and change my clothes," she replied. "Do you think I want Sam to see me—and smell me—up close after an hour under those hot lights?"

"Do you think he'll care?" Gavin tapped her forehead. "Think, lass. Use your wits. You're going to take off your clothes and get in the shower *before* you're with Sam? The stage lights must have addled your brain."

A slow grin spread across Tessa's face. "I'll get my house keys. You find the limo driver."

"That's more like it." Gavin winked at her. "Don't forget to send the limo back, though."

"You better tell the driver yourself," Tessa said. "It might slip my mind." Gavin's wicked chuckle followed her as she ran to the dressing room.

"The keys," Tessa muttered feverishly, "where did I put them?" Not on the dressing table, not on the sink in the bathroom. Not in the couch cushions, not in her jacket.

The muted sound of a lone guitar seeped through the door. *Flamenco,* Tessa thought distractedly, wondering which one of the boys from the group had branched out into Spanish music.

"My jeans!" She scrambled through the pockets and found them at last. She ran out the door and slammed it behind her.

The music was clearer now, intricate and lovely. Tessa glanced toward the front of the room and did a double take. The guitar player wasn't one of the band members, but an orderly from the hospital.

"Juan?" Tessa blinked, wondering what Juan Rodriguez was doing at an *Uprising* party. Still, stranger things had happened at post-concert parties. Much stranger.

She headed toward the exit and was stopped again, this time by incredulous laughter and exclamations.

"Who the hell is the guy in the bullfighter's suit?"

The speaker's companion shook her head. "I don't know, but I sure wish I did. He's hot!"

Tessa looked back at Juan. He had been joined by a man wearing a matador's suit of lights. Obviously, stranger things were happening.

The man held up his hands. "Ladies and gentlemen, may I have your attention?"

The party, Tessa realized, had now officially moved into the realm of much stranger. The man was Sam.

Her heart leaped to her throat. Was he drunk? Was he having some sort of breakdown? Tessa searched for the fastest way to the front of the room. She had to reach him before the security guards did.

"Although I don't have even a small percentage of the musical talent assembled here tonight," Sam continued, "I'd like you to bear with me while I sing a very special song that I wrote for a very special lady." He cleared his throat. "Juan, if you please."

Juan twanged one note on the guitar and waited patiently while Sam's voice hunted up and down the scale, trying to match it.

Tessa began to wonder if she was the one having a psychotic break. Sam? Singing? In public? It had to be a hallucination. Caused by stress, probably.

Sam and Juan finally reached a mutually agreeable note. Sam began singing, with Juan playing the melody one note at a time, a musical guide dog for this admittedly tone deaf man.

"Please don't go. My heart's full of woe."

Some people laughed. Others winced. The less polite covered their ears. Tessa stared in disbelief.

"I have to let you know, that I love you so."

A young man with a dozen earrings and a pony tail shook his head enviously. "A guy in a bullfighter's suit singing a parody of Three Blind Mice with a flamenco guitar accompanist. That's so cutting edge!"

"What it is," his buddy replied. "is lousy singing."

Tessa laid a hand on each speaker's shoulder. "Shut up," she explained, never taking her eyes off Sam.

"If you go away, I will follow you.

There's nothing on earth that I'd rather do."

Sam's face was as red as the toy poodle he had won for Tessa at the amusement park, but he kept on singing.

"I hope you can see that my love is true.

So please don't go."

The song ended and Sam's gaze finally connected with Tessa's, a homing beacon drawing her towards him.

"The lady I wrote this song for deserves much better," Sam said, blue fire gleaming in the depths of his eyes.

The crowd grew still as Juan's nimble fingers caressed the guitar strings in a slow, passionate melody.

Sam reached out toward Tessa. "But this is all I can do, other than thanking her for showing me the healing power of music, and asking her to let me love her forever."

Tessa put her hand in his and Sam drew her into his arms.

Flossie's voice rang out from the crowd. "Kiss him, Tessa, so he can't sing anymore!"

Tessa obliged and dimly heard an "Awwwwww!" of approval from the crowd.

"Will you, Tessa?" Sam murmured against her lips. "Will you let me love you?"

"You missed the song I wrote for you, Sam. The one that says I love you and will follow you wherever you go."

Sam shook his head. "You're the only one who's going anywhere. I heard that you'll be touring with the group."

"Just for a few weeks. Gavin thought it would be fun, and I thought that if you were going full time with the Air Force. . . ."

"I didn't take their offer." He threaded his fingers through her hair. "As a matter of fact, I'm making a major career change."

Tessa leaned back and looked him up and down. "You're going to be a bullfighter?" She slanted a mischievous look at him.

"I'm a troubadour," he said firmly.

"Not too much future in the troubadour game," she said. "Especially if you don't have the right wardrobe."

"Knock it off, will you?" Sam tweaked her nose. "I'm applying for a residency in trauma medicine. I figure I'll get all the challenge I'll ever need in that specialty." He paused for another kiss, and the crowd sighed again. "Will you mind being married to a resident for a few years?"

"Will you mind being married to a rock singer for one month every few years?"

Sam put his lips close to her ear. "Not if you wear your working clothes around the house occasionally."

This time Tessa kissed Sam, thoroughly and carefully. The sighs from the crowd approached hurricane force.

"Are you sure about all this, Sam?" Tessa looked up at him, searching his eyes. "Should you leave the pararescue unit? I know trauma medicine will be a challenge, but will you miss the adventure and excitement?"

"I'll never run out of either one as long as we're together." Sam swooped Tessa off her feet and carried her toward the exit, accompanied by the crowds' cheers and a last brilliant burst of guitar music.